TRUST IN LOVE

The black Mazda RX 7 in front of me stopped suddenly, and I had to hit my own brakes so hard the engine died. A boy jumped out of the car and came running over.

"I might have known," he said, looking disgusted. "A woman driver."

I stuck my head through the window and glared up at him. "I suppose it's okay for men drivers to slam on their brakes with no warning!"

"Take it easy," he said. "No harm done. Anyway, I was only kidding about the woman driver bit. Are you okay?"

He hadn't *sounded* as if he was teasing, but now that I could see him at eye level, it was impossible to stay angry. His dark hair was short and spiky above his soft brownish eyes, and his smile was wide and mischievous. I began to wish that I hadn't lost my temper. "Yeah," I said, finally smiling apologetica⸻ ⸻⸻ ⸻⸻ up a little."

His smil⸻ ⸻⸻ ⸻⸻ u're Vicki Keny⸻ ⸻⸻ you around at ⸻⸻ ⸻r."

He was ⸻ ⸻⸻ ⸻⸻ ys at school. "I know," I said.

Bantam Sweet Dreams Romances
Ask your bookseller for the books you have missed

Sweet Dreams Specials

Trust in Love

Shan Finney

BANTAM BOOKS
TORONTO • NEW YORK • LONDON • SYDNEY • AUCKLAND

RL 6, IL age 11 and up

TRUST IN LOVE

A Bantam Book / June 1988

Cover photo by Pat Hill.

ISBN 0-553-27229-2

Published simultaneously in the United States and Canada

*Bantam Books are published by Bantam Books, a division
of Bantam Doubleday Dell Publishing Group, Inc. Its
trademark, consisting of the words "Bantam Books" and
the portrayal of a rooster, is Registered in U.S. Patent and
Trademark Office and in other countries. Marca Registrada.
Bantam Books, 666 Fifth Avenue, New York, New York
10103.*

PRINTED IN THE UNITED STATES OF AMERICA

O   0 9 8 7 6 5 4 3 2 1

Trust in Love

Chapter One

As soon as we drove out of Los Angeles International Airport and merged onto the freeway to go home, everyone suddenly stopped talking. The silence was devastating. Even I, Vicki Kenyon, was at a loss for words! None of my friends would have believed it.

I glanced at Karin Eide beside me and ordered my mouth to start moving. "I'll bet you're tired," I heard myself say. "It must have been a long flight from Norway."

Karin nodded. She had just arrived to spend the year with me as a foreign exchange student. I couldn't help staring at her huge blue eyes and thinking how fabulous they were.

Or how fabulous it was going to be to have her live with us.

"It was a very long trip," she said. "But now that I am here, it seems not so tiring."

I smiled sympathetically. "That's good. You're going to love Southern California."

Karin nodded again. I brushed my shoulder-length auburn hair back from my face and looked out the car window. The late-August sun seemed dim through the light layer of smog that almost always hung over the free-way. Tall buildings and tract houses swept by in a hazy blur, but I hardly noticed the scenery. All I could think about was how Karin Eide's arrival would change my life.

Normally, for instance, I would have been alone in the backseat. That was just *one* haz-ard of being an only child. Some kids envied me for not having brothers or sisters, but I thought they were crazy. Of course, there were some definite advantages, such as my own bathroom, a private telephone, a decent al-lowance, and the use of my mom's car almost any time I wanted it.

But there were a lot of negatives, too. The adults in my house always outnumbered me two to one. My parents were fairly enlight-ened, but they were still parents, and there were some things they just couldn't understand.

For instance, they'd never understood how lonely I felt, being the only kid, or at least they hadn't done anything about it. At times, though, I wondered if that was my fault. I wouldn't make even third runner-up in a contest for the world's best daughter, mainly because I've always had a mind of my own. Maybe my parents had decided not to have more children because they were afraid of getting another one like me.

Deep in my heart I knew that that idea was ridiculous. My parents obviously loved me. They always took an interest in what I was doing and gave me almost everything I wanted. The trouble was that what I *really* wanted was a sister close to my own age. A twin would have been perfect.

Of course, it was too late for that, but having Karin Eide come to stay with me was almost as good. Even though I was from the United States and she was from Norway, we were both sixteen and that meant we had to have a lot in common.

I turned back to Karin, hoping she was as happy to be here as I was to have her. "I can't wait to show you around," I said. "All this probably seems like the Twilight Zone to you

3

right now." She gave me a perplexed look, and I realized she didn't know what I was talking about. "I mean, everything must seem strange," I explained.

"Strange, yes," Karin said. "But a good kind of strange, I think." She smiled doubtfully. "It makes me a little nervous, though, coming to such a big city."

I stared at her in surprise. For weeks, I'd tried to imagine what she would be like. I had almost expected her to show up with long blond braids and a handmade Norwegian sweater on, but Karin's appearance was nothing like that. Her light blond hair looked great in a stylish blunt cut, and she was wearing a blue miniskirt that I was already dying to borrow.

From the first moment I saw Karin, I'd been delighted at how sophisticated and confident she seemed. Now I could hardly believe she was really nervous about living in Southern California. "I thought you were used to being in a big city," I said. "Isn't Oslo the capital of Norway?"

Karin laughed. "The capital, yes, and for Norway, Oslo is a major city. But it has many farms and forests and hills. Here in Anaheim, you see only streets and buildings."

"I see what you mean," I said. "But actually, we're not too far from the ocean. And we've been passing a lot of different towns. We're just coming to Anaheim, and it isn't all that big."

"That is good news," Karin replied, rolling her eyes comically. She sounded so relieved that I suddenly felt protective of her. "Don't worry," I said reassuringly. "You'll get used to it. Besides, I'll be around to help you."

Karin looked really grateful, and I was surprised at how good that made me feel. In the past, I'd never had to think about anyone but myself. Now I'd be looking out for Karin, too. That idea didn't bother me at all. With Karin as my new sister, my junior year was going to be great.

I had a feeling the year was going to be wonderful in other ways, too, and one of them included Jeff Shafer. I'd seen him around before, but we hadn't really noticed each other until a week earlier at the car wash.

Jeff was in line ahead of me in his black Mazda RX 7, when he suddenly slammed on his brakes, almost causing me to rear-end him. I had to hit my own brakes so hard that I killed the engine of my mother's Toyota. Jeff jumped out of his car and came running over to me.

"I might have known," he said, looking disgusted. "A woman driver."

I stuck my head through the window and glared up at him. "I suppose it's okay for men drivers to slam on their brakes with no warning." I was so furious that my face was quickly turning bright red. Jeff had practically forced me to run into him, and then he had the gall to act superior! I could hardly believe it.

Jeff stared at me for a moment, then glanced at the bumper of his car. "Take it easy," he said. "No harm done. Anyway, I was only teasing about the woman driver bit." Suddenly he smiled and leaned toward me, propping his elbows on the window of the Toyota. "Sorry," he said. "I wasn't paying attention, I guess. Are you okay?"

He hadn't *sounded* as if he was teasing, but now that I could see him at eye level, it was impossible to stay angry. Jeff's dark hair was short and spiky above his soft brownish eyes, and his smile was wide and mischievous. I began to wish that I hadn't lost my temper. "Yeah," I said, finally smiling apologetically. "It just shook me up a little."

Jeff's smile widened irresistibly. "You're Vicki Kenyon, aren't you? I've seen you around at Greeley High. I'm Jeff Shafer."

"I know," I said. "Junior varsity basketball.

And this year you'll be a senior, so you'll probably play varsity."

Jeff looked surprised and pleased. "You noticed? Most kids don't pay much attention to basketball players. The football team gets all the publicity. You must be a real sports fan."

I shrugged casually. "Not really. I go to some of the games. School spirit, and all that."

Jeff nodded, as if I had said something deep. His chin jutted forward, and I saw a dimple there that I hadn't noticed before. The silence was beginning to feel awkward. "So," I said, "it's your turn to say something."

Jeff laughed. "Thanks. I was so overwhelmed, I lost my place in the conversation for a second. Somehow I always had you figured more for the brain brigade than the pep squad."

I knew he was teasing again, but I didn't like being stereotyped. The fact that I got good grades didn't make me a grind. "Yeah, and I always figured you for a dumb jock," I retorted, hoping he would get the message.

He gave me a long look, then grinned again and threw up his hands in surrender. "Okay, okay. I guess I've met my match."

I heard a horn honking behind me. "We'd better get going," I said regretfully. "We're holding up the line."

Jeff glanced at the car behind me. "Right.

But this is only round one. Good things might happen."

"Sure," I had replied. "And little green men could drop in from outer space."

On the way home from the airport, I almost groaned out loud at the memory. At the time, I'd thought I was so clever, but now I wished I hadn't sounded so sarcastic. Secretly, I had agreed with Jeff that good things *could* happen between us.

It was intriguing, anyway, I decided as my dad turned the car off the freeway and headed into Anaheim. I hadn't really meant to put Jeff off at all, but the words just tumbled out. That was one of my problems; I had a quick tongue and often said things I didn't mean in an effort to be witty. Maybe Jeff understood that since he obviously liked to kid around, too. But what if he didn't?

Before I had time to consider that question, I saw the neon sign for Guido's Pizza Parlor flashing up ahead. "There's Guido's," I told Karin, pointing out the window. "A lot of kids from the neighborhood hang out there. Greeley High is two blocks away."

Five minutes later my dad pulled into the driveway in front of our four-bedroom brick house. "Well, here we are," he announced, looking over his shoulder at Karin. "I'll bet you're glad to have your feet on solid ground again."

Karin smiled and nodded. "Yes. I am very happy to be here." She climbed out of the car and glanced around at the neighborhood, with its sprawling houses, neat lawns, and big shade trees. "It is almost as I imagined," she said in her melodic Norwegian accent. "But very much more quiet."

"It won't seem that way for long," I told her. "There'll be a lot more activity around here after school starts next week." I lifted Karin's large suitcase and a nylon bag out of the car trunk. "Come on, I'll show you your room."

Karin grabbed two more bags and followed me into the house, across the living room, and down the hallway. "Such a big house!" she exclaimed. "I was afraid of making you feel crowded by adding another person."

The idea that Karin could make me feel crowded seemed so preposterous that I nearly giggled. "That's one thing you definitely don't have to worry about," I said. "We have four bedrooms. Yours and mine are down here. My mom and dad sleep at the other end of the house."

I opened the door to the room at the end of the hall and waited for Karin to go in. "This used to be a guest room," I explained. "But lately it was filled with all sorts of junk before we fixed it up for you."

"But it is so beautiful," Karin said, looking around happily. "You should not have gone to so much trouble."

I shrugged. My mom and I had worked hard on the room, painting the walls a soft lilac color and buying a new comforter in blue, beige, and lilac. The soft colors, along with the antique oak dresser and white lace curtains, gave the room a cozy, old-fashioned charm.

Personally, I preferred a more modern look, but my mom had thought Karin might like a more traditional style. Seeing how much she liked the room made all our work seem worthwhile. "It wasn't any trouble," I said. "Actually, it was fun."

Karin smiled. "I'm lucky to come to such a nice home."

"*I'm* the one who's lucky," I said. "I'm so glad you're here." I flopped onto the bed, but I was so restless that I jumped up instantly and walked over to the closet. "It's not very big," I said, opening the sliding door. "Come on, I'll help you unpack."

"I don't know where to begin," Karin said.

She opened the largest suitcase and began taking out piles of clothes.

I wasn't sure where to begin, either, but I picked up a stack of sweaters and carried them to the dresser. Suddenly, I stopped in my tracks and held up a pink sweater with a silver thread woven through it. "Wow, this is too much!"

Karen looked up from the suitcase with a perplexed smile. "Too much means—what do you say—flashy?"

For a second, we stared at each other in confusion, then all at once I understood. "No!" I exclaimed, shaking my head. "This sweater is definitely not flashy. 'Too much' means too good to be true."

Karin laughed. "I think I understand."

"You'll catch on fast. I know everything must seem strange to you now, but you're not going to have any trouble fitting in here."

I meant it, too. When I'd persuaded my parents to sign us up as a host family, I hadn't known whether we would be chosen, or whether we would be getting a boy or girl. As it turned out, I couldn't have found a better "sister" if I'd picked her out of a mail-order catalog.

"It's going to be great having you here," I said sincerely. "We can swap clothes and

11

double-date and—" I stopped abruptly when I realized that I'd started using jargon again. "Do you say 'double-date' in Norway?"

"Not in exactly those words," Karin said, hanging a dress in the closet. "But I think that how we do it is the same."

Talking about double dating had made me think of Jeff again. Introducing Karin would give me a good excuse to talk to him again soon.

"There's this guy, Jeff Shafer, who's a senior at Greeley High," I began. "We haven't ever dated, but I have a feeling we will soon." I caught myself grinning like an idiot as I remembered Jeff's mischievous expression and warm brown eyes.

"From the look on your face, he must be wonderful," said Karin. "I would like to meet him."

"Jeff is more than wonderful. He's a basketball player, so he probably knows lots of cute guys. We can fix you up for dates if I get together with him."

Karin gave me a funny look, and I instantly realized my mistake. My face was so red with embarrassment that I must have looked like I was wearing clown makeup. "Not that you need to be fixed up," I said quickly. "Half the guys at school are going to be hitting on you for dates, I guarantee."

Karin gave a small laugh. "It's not that," she said. "It is that I already have a boyfriend who waits for me in Oslo. His name is Niels, and he is—as you say—more than wonderful."

I stared at her for a moment, taking in her perfect complexion, trim figure, and gorgeous big blue eyes. Why hadn't it ever occurred to me that she might already have a boyfriend? "It figures," I said, shaking my head at my own stupidity. "I should have guessed that you would already be spoken for."

Karin blushed at the compliment. "I hope that will not spoil our fun together."

"No way!" I said firmly. Secretly, I *was* a little disappointed that my plans for double dating had fallen through. But at the same time, I had to admit that I felt a bit relieved to learn that Karin Eide wasn't available.

Chapter Two

When Nancy Davis called at eleven o'clock on Saturday morning, I was still in bed. Nancy and I had been best friends since junior high, and now I could hardly wait to introduce her to Karin. "Where have you been?" I asked. "I tried to call you all day yesterday."

"I went waterskiing with Gary."

She said it so calmly that I wasn't sure I'd heard her right. Nancy and Gary had been going together forever, until last Fourth of July when they'd had a fight and broken up. Since then, they'd been avoiding each other. "You're kidding," I said at last. "I thought you and Gary weren't even speaking."

"I know," Nancy said. "I'm as surprised as you are."

I could tell that she was more excited than she sounded. Nancy always tried to be sensible about boys, but I'd known all along that she still loved Gary. "So," I said, trying to sound as casual as she did. "Does this mean you're getting back together?"

"Maybe," she said cautiously. "Let's go out to Newport Beach this afternoon and I'll tell you all about it."

"Great!" I said. "You'll get to meet Karin. I was trying to think of somewhere to take her today. Wait a minute while I ask her if she wants to go."

Nancy groaned. "Couldn't I meet her tomorrow? I mean, talking about my love life is kind of personal."

Considering that I'd been waiting to introduce Karin and Nancy since Thursday night, Nancy's lack of enthusiasm was a little upsetting. "You don't have to worry about Karin," I said. "She's terrific. We're getting along great; and I just know you're going to like her."

"Sure," Nancy said. "But that's not the point."

I sighed. I could understand Nancy's wanting to talk to me alone, but she was putting me in a very difficult situation. "Come on," I said, "I can't abandon Karin on her second full day in California. Besides, I really want you to meet her."

"Oh, all right," Nancy agreed finally. "I'll pick you up in about an hour, okay?"

I hung up the phone feeling pleased. But later, when we got to the beach, I started wondering if I'd made a mistake.

The day was unusually hot, but none of us felt like going in the water yet. Karin started spreading our beach towels on the sand while I helped Nancy set up her pink and blue striped umbrella. She hadn't said a word yet about Gary, and I was getting impatient. "Okay," I said, "tell me about yesterday."

Nancy glanced at Karin and said, "It can wait."

Right then, I should have known that Karin was going to change my life in more ways than I'd imagined. But it didn't make any difference. I was responsible for Karin, and my friends would just have to accept her.

"Stop being so mysterious," I told Nancy, flopping down on my towel. "The last I heard, you never wanted to see Gary again, so how did you guys end up waterskiing?"

Nancy laughed. "You won't believe it," she said, "but he almost ran me down on his skateboard. And then it was as if we'd never been mad at each other. Gary—" She stopped and glanced at Karin again.

Karin smiled and said, "Gary is your boyfriend?"

"No," Nancy said. "I mean, maybe, but I don't know."

I could see from Karin's expression that she was pretty confused. "Gary and Nancy used to go steady," I explained. "But they broke up."

Nancy nodded. "So," she continued, "he came shooting around a corner at the mall, and then his skateboard went flying out from under him. He practically fell into my arms before I—"

Karin was looking confused again, and I interrupted Nancy to explain about skateboards. "So what happened then?" I asked, turning back to Nancy.

"As I was saying, he practically fell into my arms before I even saw who he was. Then we were looking into each other's eyes, and he got this funny smile on his face. . . ."

"They hadn't even spoken to each other for months," I told Karin.

"Yeah," Nancy said. She sounded a bit exasperated, probably because of all my interruptions, and I couldn't really blame her. I was starting to feel like a Ping-Pong ball, bouncing back and forth between the two of them.

"It's a long story," I said to Karin. I turned back to Nancy again and said, "Maybe you should fill her in."

That must have been the last straw, because Nancy rolled her eyes and shrugged. "Never mind, we'll talk about it later." There were a few moments of awkward silence, and then she said, "Want to go get a hamburger?"

I was starving, so I jumped right up and brushed the sand off my beach thongs. The three of us walked over to the hamburger stand, where a lot of kids were waiting to buy snacks. As I made my way through the crowd, a Frisbee flew toward me and I reached up to catch it. Suddenly a guy's arm snaked out in front of me and grabbed for it, and I froze in my tracks.

Even though I couldn't see his face, I was almost certain that the guy was Jeff Shafer. I hadn't expected to see him until school started next Tuesday, but here he was standing six feet away from me!

I sneaked up behind him, stood on my toes, and put my hands over his eyes. "Guess who," I said, trying to disguise my voice.

Jeff started to turn around, then stopped and stood still. "Cyndi Lauper," he said. "The A-Team. Goldilocks."

I giggled. "Nope."

At that point, Jeff grabbed my wrists and spun to face me. He was wearing the same mischievous smile I remembered from the car wash. "Zo," he said, in a phony foreign accent. "Ve meet again, Vicki Kenyon!"

Suddenly I didn't feel like kidding around anymore. Jeff was still holding on to my wrists, and his fingers felt warm and strong against my skin. I gazed into his fabulous brown eyes.

Jeff let go of my wrists, but he kept looking at me with his funny smile. "Hi," he said.

"Hi," I replied numbly. I couldn't think of anything else to say.

Fortunately, Nancy and Karin came up just then, giving me a chance to introduce everyone.

"Hi," Jeff said, shaking hands with Karin. "I heard Vicki had a foreign exchange student coming to stay with her. That's really great."

"It is nice to be here," Karin replied. "Vicki told me that you are a big basketball star at Greeley High School."

"Hmm," Jeff said, giving me a funny look. "What else did Vicki say about me?"

I held my breath, wondering if she would actually tell him everything I had said about him. Then she smiled teasingly and said, "I should think that is enough, yes? Not everyone is known to be a big basketball star."

Jeff laughed. "I'm not really a star. It just looks that way because I play center. They put tall guys like me under the basket, but the guards and forwards do most of the work."

"I see," Karin said. "Then you are not so good a player as Vicki thinks?" From the way she narrowed her eyes, I almost thought she was flirting with him, but that was a ridiculous idea. She probably just didn't know anything about basketball.

"Oh, I'm all right," Jeff said. "When they give me the ball, I can usually turn it into points."

"Hey, Shafer!" someone yelled. "You want mustard on this dog, or not?"

"The works," Jeff called back. "I'm with some other guys," he said turning to me. "I'd better get going."

"Okay," I said. "It was nice seeing you."

"Yeah, I'm glad we ran into each other again."

"Very funny," I said. "But if you don't mind, I'd like to forget about your bad driving and move on to something else."

Jeff grinned. "Listen," he said, after a moment. "I've got to go, but maybe we'll come over and join you, okay? Where are you camped?"

"Over by the second lifeguard station." I glanced at Nancy, wondering if she'd mind having the boys join us. She *had* wanted to be alone today. I was a little surprised when she nodded and said, "Look for the pink-and-blue umbrella."

"Are you sure it's all right with you?" I asked her a few minutes later, as we walked back to our towels carrying hamburgers and sodas.

Nancy tucked a wisp of dark brown hair behind her ear and shrugged. "What's a little more company? Besides, it will give Karin a chance to get acquainted with some other kids before school starts."

I could tell from her voice that she was being sincere, and the sudden change in her attitude toward Karin surprised me. But it shouldn't have, I scolded myself. Nancy never stayed upset for long. That was one of the things I admired most about her—she could easily put her own feelings aside and think about other people.

Once Nancy had accepted Karin's being with us, things went along more easily. I asked her again if she and Gary were getting back together, and she told us about their date while we ate our hamburgers.

21

"So," I said, "what is the story? Are you guys in love again?"

Nancy looked thoughtful. "I think so, but we have a lot to talk about. We're not going to jump back into anything."

"Being apart makes you think about so many things, no?" Karin said sympathetically. "Sometimes I wonder how it will be when I return to Niels after a year away."

"Is Niels your steady boyfriend?" Nancy asked.

"He was," Karin said. "I only hope that he will be still when I return."

"He'd have to be crazy not to wait for you," I said. Compared to Nancy and me, Karin looked like a model or movie star. Nancy was pretty but kind of short, with dark hair and a slim, boyish figure. I was about three inches taller with reddish-brown hair. But Karin just had something extra. I couldn't help envying someone as beautiful as Karin, no matter how much I liked her.

Suddenly, once again, I spotted a red Frisbee sailing toward me. I jumped up and grabbed it with one hand, then looked up to see Jeff Shafer waiting for me to throw it back. Instead, I threw a sideways slice to one of the three other boys who were with him. Then Nancy and Karin got up and joined the game. We all ran around chasing and tossing the Frisbee until we were hot and sweaty.

"I think I am ready to try the water," Karin said, lifting her damp hair off her forehead.

"I'll second that," Jeff said. He ran toward the ocean, and the rest of us followed, racing one another to the surf.

The beach was crowded, but there weren't too many swimmers. Most people don't spend much time in the water because, even on hot days, the Pacific Ocean is cold. I usually go in for short dips, but this time I stayed in a bit longer, splashing around with the other kids and body surfing on the small waves.

Just when I was about half-frozen and figured everyone else was, too, Karin started swimming toward deeper water. Jeff joined her, and the rest of us went back to our towels.

It seemed as if Jeff and Karin were gone forever. By the time I spotted them running across the sand toward us, fog was rolling in and the sun looked pale. Jeff flopped down on my towel and began rubbing his head with one corner of it. "So much for dumb jocks," he said. "I went along with Karin to play lifeguard, and I couldn't get within twenty feet of her."

"That is because you did not grow up swimming in Oslo Fjord," Karin said, pulling on her beach jacket. "Compared to Norway, California is hot like an oven."

"That's what *you* think!" Jeff teased. "Is Norway really as cold and dark as I think it is?"

"For an American—maybe, yes. But if you were Norwegian, you would say it is crisp and bracing." She raised both arms and flexed her muscles. The gesture was so comical that everyone laughed.

"Somehow, it's hard to think of you as a bodybuilder," Jeff said, still grinning. "But you are a powerful swimmer. You ought to try out for the Greeley swim team."

"That's a good idea," I said, mostly to remind them that I was still there. I wanted my friends to like Karin, of course, but she and Jeff were getting along so well that I was beginning to wonder just how much *he* liked her.

Nancy must have had the same idea, because she gave me a curious look. A moment later, she started getting her things together. "I hate to be a wet blanket, but I have a date to get ready for," she said.

"Yeah, me, too," said one of Jeff's friends. "It looks like we've used up our share of rays, anyway."

Feeling a sudden chill, I reached for my T-shirt. After the way Jeff had teased me at the hamburger stand, I'd thought he might ask me for a date. Now we were getting ready to leave, and he still hadn't said anything— not to me, anyway. He had spent most of the day talking to Karin, and who knew *what* he'd said to her?

Casually, I packed my beach bag and went to help Nancy fold the umbrella. Everybody said good-bye, and Nancy, Karin, and I started walking toward the parking lot. Then Jeff called my name.

I stopped and looked over my shoulder. He ran toward me, then skidded to a stop as I turned to meet him. "I almost forgot," he said, looking straight into my eyes. "I'd like you to come to my back-to-school-party next Saturday night. What do you say?"

I was so stunned that I could hardly answer. Finally, I managed to say, "Sure, that'd be fun."

"Great," he said. "Bring Karin and Nancy, too."

My heart sank. I'd thought he was inviting just me. But then he squeezed my hand and added, "I'll be looking forward to it, then. But maybe we'll run into each other again before next Saturday."

"I'll probably see you at school next week," I heard myself say.

"Sure," he said. "And little green men . . ." We both burst out laughing.

"I guess I'll never hear the end of that," I said, wrinkling my nose at him.

Jeff shrugged and gave my hand another squeeze. "See you around."

"Yeah, see you around."

He left me standing there, wondering how I could have been so stupid as to think he and Karin had been flirting with each other.

I still had a lot to learn about being a "sister," I decided, and besides, I knew I didn't own Jeff. Fortunately, Karin couldn't know what I'd been thinking about her and Jeff. Right then, I was so happy about the way things were turning out that I promised myself I would make it up to her anyway.

Chapter Three

The halls at Greeley High were always a disaster area the first few days of school. By Thursday, most of us had memorized our classrooms and locker combinations, but things hadn't really calmed down yet. At noon, when I left my English class to meet Nancy for lunch, all I could see was a mass of heads and shoulders. Kids were milling around everywhere, catching up on summer news, making dates, or choosing new activities for the year.

Trying to spot Nancy in the crowd was impossible, so I leaned against a locker and hoped she'd find me soon. I was thinking about signing up as a tutor in English as a second language, and I had a meeting to get to. But before the meeting, I had to get to the cafeteria, check up on Karin, and grab a sandwich to take with me.

I'd been busy for the last three days showing Karin around and explaining how we did things. It was fun being with her. At night we did the dishes together, then sat around talking or playing records in my room. At school, Karin was a major attraction, and running around with her kept me pretty busy. In fact, my schedule was so tight that I had begun to wonder if tutoring might be a mistake. Hosting a foreign exchange student was a big responsibility, and I hadn't really planned to take on any other extracurricular activities this year.

But having Karin live with me was also what had gotten me interested in English as a second language, or ESL. My experiences with Karin had helped me understand some of the problems of having to communicate in a foreign language. Although Karin spoke English very well, I was aware of the difficulties she was having. I didn't have to sign up to tutor until after the informational meeting, so I decided to wait and make up my mind then.

Just as I had given up on Nancy and started

walking toward the door at the end of the hall, she finally caught up with me. "Sorry I'm late," she said. "Daryl Sullivan just asked me to go to the movies with him tomorrow night."

I raised my eyebrows. "What did you tell him?"

"I said 'yes,' of course."

As usual, Nancy seemed so casual that I wasn't sure I'd heard her right. "Are you crazy?" I asked finally. "What about you and Gary?"

"We're not officially going together, you know." She looked at me as though that one sentence explained everything. Nancy reminded me of my biology teacher, Mrs. Conrad, when she was answering a question that she thought was very obvious.

"But you still love him, don't you?" I asked.

"Yeah," Nancy replied. "I can't let that stop me from seeing other guys, though. Gary and I agreed we're not going steady, and if I started acting as if we were, I'd expect him to do the same. I mean, what if I stopped dating and then saw Gary with some other girl?"

"You'd be jealous," I said cautiously. "If you still loved him."

"*Exactly!*" She emphasized the word as if I'd just guessed the winning lottery number.

That was a pretty good sign that I wasn't going to like what she said next.

"So," Nancy went on, "if I keep dating other people, I won't have to get jealous."

"What does that have to do with anything?" I said. "I'd be just as upset whether I was dating other guys or not."

"Well, I wouldn't," Nancy said. "Seeing Gary with someone else might hurt, but I can't get mad at him for doing the same thing I'm doing."

We left the building and started down the walk toward the cafeteria. The day was so warm and sunny that I wanted to take off my sandals and walk barefoot in the grass. I heard someone yell my name, and I turned around to see Jeff Shafer jogging to catch up with us.

"Hi," I said.

Jeff smiled and nodded toward the cafeteria. "I was just on my way to lunch. What about you?" The sunlight brought out reddish highlights in his hair, and his teeth looked extra white against his dark tan. I tend to notice details like that and I must have been staring, because suddenly Jeff stopped smiling. "What, have I got something on my teeth?"

I wrinkled my nose. "Yuck, no. I was admiring your tan."

He looked at Nancy and rolled his eyes toward me. "Is she always like this?"

"Yeah," Nancy said. "You have to get used to her. Oh, look," she added, giving me her three's-a-crowd look. "There's Sally. I'm going to say hi."

She walked away before either of us had time to object. That was another nice thing about Nancy: she could be very tactful. Jeff and I watched her leave, then stood around trying to think of something to say. The silence was a bit awkward, but on the other hand, I could have stood there all day, looking into Jeff's eyes. Then I remembered that I was supposed to be in a hurry.

"I've got to check on Karin and grab a sandwich," I told him. "I have a meeting in fifteen minutes, for tutoring in English— "

"As a second language," Jeff finished for me. "I think you'd be really good at that."

"Thanks," I said, shifting my books to my other arm and starting toward the cafeteria again. "So, how are your classes going so far?"

"Not bad," Jeff said. "I'm taking less math and more history and government. I'm thinking about studying political science next year in college."

"You're kidding!" I took in his tall, slim

build and the muscles. "I would have thought you'd have a career in sports," I said.

He gave me a funny look, somewhere between a smile and a frown. "Just another dumb jock, huh?"

He was throwing back my words at the car wash again, and my face turned bright red. He was teasing, but I could tell he was also serious. Why did I always get so confused whenever I started talking to him?

"I didn't really think you were a dumb jock," I said. "I was only trying to get my point across."

"Oh. And what point was that?" Jeff gave me a hard look, as though he really expected an answer.

The car wash incident had happened at least two weeks earlier. I couldn't even remember what else I'd said then. I looked up at him and frowned. "It doesn't matter. Maybe we should just forget the car wash."

After a second, Jeff's face broke into a gorgeous smile. "I will if you will. Are you still coming to my party Saturday night?"

I nodded and began to walk a little faster. "Definitely. So are Karin and Nancy."

"Great!" he said. "I hope you like to dance."

"More than anything—except maybe arguing with hotshot basketball players."

Jeff laughed. "I bet we'd dance really well together."

I know we would, I thought, as I pushed open the cafeteria door. I didn't dare say anything. Instead, I smiled at Jeff over my shoulder and said, "I guess we'll find out."

The cafeteria was jammed with kids, laughing and talking and shooting baskets with their empty lunch bags. We found Karin at the center of a crowd of my friends. She was so busy laughing that she barely looked up when Jeff and I joined the group. "Hi," I said loudly. "I thought I'd stop by and see how you're doing."

"I was wondering what became of you," Karin said, looking up with a big smile. "You didn't tell me that lunch is the best part of the day."

I could tell from her pink cheeks and sparkling eyes that Karin was really enjoying herself. She looked more gorgeous than ever in her pretty yellow pullover and gray miniskirt.

But what really added most to her attractiveness was her easy way of joking and flirting. Bantering in a foreign language must be very difficult, but Karin was doing very well. She seemed to have a knack for putting everyone instantly at ease.

I was honestly glad to see Karin having such a good time, but I had to admit it bothered me a little, too. The idea of looking out for Karin had made me feel special. Now it turned out that she didn't really need my help. In fact, she was so popular that I didn't see any point in sticking around much longer. "I have to get going," I announced. "See you later."

Karin threw me a quick smile and nodded. "I will see you in history," she said, referring to the only class we had together.

"Sorry you have to rush off," Jeff said. "I'll walk over to the snack bar with you."

That made me feel a little better, and I gave him a grateful smile. "You must be starving," I said. "I know I am, anyway."

Jeff shrugged. "Yeah, I could handle a couple of steaks, maybe three or four baked potatoes. Then I'd top it off with a pineapple sundae and a slab of chocolate cake." He rubbed his stomach and smacked his lips. "We jocks are big eaters, you know."

"Not that big," I said, laughing. "Or you wouldn't be so slim."

"You're right," Jeff replied. "So I'll just grab a sandwich and go sit with Karin while you're at your meeting."

The thought of Jeff and Karin eating lunch

without me was enough to make me lose my appetite. I bought a tuna salad sandwich anyway, then said good-bye to Jeff and hurried to the meeting.

On the way, I tried to think about Jeff's party, but I couldn't get Karin out of my mind. All my life, I'd wanted a sister. Now I had the next best thing, and it was starting to look as if I was resenting her.

It wasn't Karin's fault. She was doing exactly what I'd hoped she would—fitting in and having a good time. I'd wanted her to like Jeff, then I got jealous when they hit it off well. Now she was popular with my friends, and I felt left out.

Stop it, I told myself. Karin was going to be living with me for the entire year. *I* was the one who had invited her, and I was supposed to be happy about it. I was going to have to quit resenting Karin's popularity and try not to be jealous of her and Jeff. But if she ever *did* decide to move in on Jeff, I promised myself that was where I'd draw the line.

Chapter Four

On Saturday evening before Jeff's party, Karin sat in my room, playing the same album on my stereo over and over again. She could have listened to music in the family room, but she preferred my bedroom.

The room's main attraction was that it was very private and more like a den than a bedroom. One wall was all built-in shelves, where I kept a small TV, my telephone, and the stereo. I also stored my books, albums, and knickknacks there, including my crystal ball and a stuffed Mickey Mouse that I had won at Disneyland.

When I went in to start getting ready for the party, Karin was sitting in one of my white wicker chairs. "I think we should leave about eight-fifteen," I said. "The party starts at eight, but I don't want to get there too early."

Karin reached over and turned down the the stereo. "Then it is not correct to arrive on time? I have so much yet to learn of your American customs."

I could understand why she'd asked the question, but I wasn't sure how to answer her.

"I wouldn't exactly say it's not *correct* to be on time," I said. "I mean, it would be okay if we got there at eight."

"It is a matter of personal choice, then?"

That wasn't exactly right, either. "Not always," I replied. "If it's for a dinner party, you should be on time. For informal parties, you can be more flexible. Tonight I'm feeling a little nervous, so I'd rather let other people get there first to break the ice."

Karin looked as if she still didn't understand my explanation, but I had to start getting ready. "Listen," I said, "I have to shower and do my hair. I want to look really nice tonight." I started toward the bathroom, then stuck my head back in the doorway. "Do you want to shower first?"

Karin shook her head. "I have already," she said. "The bathroom is all yours."

I was relieved to hear that, because I didn't feel like waiting for the bathroom. I took a quick shower, then blew my hair dry and reached for my curling iron. It wasn't in the drawer where it belonged, so I searched the rest of the bathroom. Finally I gave up and went to ask Karin if she'd seen it anywhere.

As soon as I entered her room, I saw her standing in front of the mirror using my curling iron on her thick bangs. I was so annoyed that I wanted to scream. "I've been looking all over for that," I said. "You could have asked me before you took it."

Karin's pale eyes seemed shocked as she looked back at me from the mirror. "I am sorry," she said, unplugging the iron and winding up the cord. "I thought you didn't use it, but it is my mistake. In the future, I will ask before I borrow."

Her apology was so sincere that I felt like a jerk. She was right—I hardly ever used the curling iron. And having it right that minute wasn't exactly a matter of life and death.

"That's okay," I said quickly. "Normally I just blow-dry my hair, but I wanted to do something special with it tonight for the party. I can wait until you're finished."

"I am done," Karin said. She smiled and held out the curling iron, but I could tell her feelings were hurt.

"I didn't mean to snap at you," I apologized. "I guess I'm all wound up about spending the evening with Jeff. I mean, if I *am* spending it with him. He never really said I'd be his date."

"Perhaps not," Karin said. "But he likes you very much. That is for anyone to see."

It was nice of her to reassure me, and I hoped that meant she'd accepted my apology. "Thanks," I said. "Have you decided what you're going to wear?"

Karin tucked her hair behind her ears and pulled some spiky curls up above her forehead. "Well, I had thought of borrowing your red sweater. To go with my black stretch pants." She glanced at me cautiously in the mirror before adding, "That is, if you had no idea of wearing it yourself."

I almost groaned out loud. I *had* been planning to wear that sweater, but I felt too guilty to say so. Since I had decided to stop being so jealous and resentful of Karin, she and I had been getting along perfectly. But tonight in only the last hour, I'd been impatient about answering her questions, I'd resented sharing the bathroom, and I'd practically accused her of stealing my curling iron. Considering how selfish I'd been, the least I could do was lend Karin my sweater.

"Actually, I was going to wear my jumpsuit," I lied. "The sweater's in my top drawer."

By the time we got to Jeff's house, I was glad I'd decided to let Karin wear my red sweater. She looked great in it, and I felt better in my jumpsuit, anyway. Karin and I checked each other over one last time, then walked up the steps and rang the doorbell. A moment later Mrs. Shafer came to the door and showed us to the downstairs recreation room.

The party was already off to a good start. The Shafers' rec room was filled with kids. Loud rock music blared from the stereo, and about a dozen couples were dancing in the middle of the room. Jeff was talking to a girl from Greeley named Wendy.

"It looks like Jeff is busy," I told Karin. "Let's look for Nancy."

We found her with a group of kids near the bowl of chips and dip. She had come to the party with Gary, and he was standing with his arm around her shoulders. "Hi, Vicki," he said, as we walked up to them. "I haven't seen you for a while."

"I know," I said and turned to Karin. "Have you and Gary ever met?"

"Sure," Gary said, smiling. "Everyone knows Karin. How's it going?"

"Fine," Karin said. "I am looking forward to my first American house party."

Suddenly I felt someone's hand on my back. Jeff was standing beside me. "It's about time you two got here," he said. "Hey, Karin, nice sweater."

"Yeah," Gary chimed in. "I was just about to say that."

Both guys stood there ogling Karin as if they were judging a beauty contest. Nancy rolled her eyes in exasperation. I just sighed. I should have known Karin would get compliments on *my* sweater. But even if I'd worn it myself, Jeff and Gary probably wouldn't have looked at me the way they were looking at Karin. She was simply gorgeous, and that was all there was to it.

"Looks like a good party," I said, trying to get the conversation moving.

Jeff grinned. "That's what I like—a girl who'll tell me what I want to hear."

Before I could think of a witty comeback, a boy named David from Karin's math class joined us. The way he smiled at Karin made me wonder if he had a crush on her. "Great sweater," he said. "Would you like to dance?"

Karin blushed. "I'm not much of a dancer to fast music."

"That's okay," David said. "I'm a first-rate teacher. You may as well take advantage of it."

Karin hesitated, looking doubtful. David held up one hand and started talking like a salesman on a late-night television commercial. "Wait! I'll make you a deal you can't refuse—my special introductory package for Norwegian exchange students only. Six free lessons—disco, ballroom, rock, special requests. And that's not all . . ."

The rest of us laughed. "I guess that is an offer I cannot refuse," Karin said. "But I think you do not know what you are in for."

"Trust me," David said, reaching for her hand. "I'll cope."

As they walked away, Jeff turned to me. "I think he's got a thing for her."

" That's just what I was thinking," I said.

Nancy nodded. "Maybe somebody ought to tell David about Niels."

Jeff gave me a questioning look. "Niels is Karin's boyfriend in Norway," I explained. "They're going steady."

Jeff let out a low whistle. "When that news

gets around, there are going to be some very disappointed dudes at Greeley High."

I couldn't help wondering if he was including himself in the category of "disappointed dudes." "Yeah," I said, trying not to sound too jealous, "she's so gorgeous she could probably have any guy she wanted."

"I don't know about that," Jeff said. "She's foxy, all right, but not everybody goes for that type." He looked into my eyes as though his words had a special meaning for me.

Just when I thought I'd melt if he didn't stop looking at me, Nancy said, "And just what type is that?"

Jeff shrugged. "Karin is beautiful and awfully nice, but she's pretty tame compared to some girls I know. Personally, I like a girl to be a bit feisty."

I was thrilled. Jeff hadn't come right out and said he liked me but I knew he thought of me as "feisty."

Then he smiled and held out his hand to me. "How about a dance?"

A new song was just beginning, so I took Jeff's hand and we made our way through the crowd.

Jeff was a terrific dancer, and eventually I relaxed and let the beat take over. All too soon, the song ended and I stood looking up at Jeff, feeling as though I had just awakened from a dream. Jeff stared back at me, smiling, and then we both burst out laughing. "I told you we'd dance well together," he said. "Was I right?"

"For once," I said. "And I'll probably never hear the end of it." I smiled to make sure he knew I was teasing, then lifted my hair off my neck where it was damp from perspiring.

"I'm hot, too," Jeff said, wiping his forehead with the back of his hand. "Let's go get something to drink."

We walked over to the refreshment table, where there was a plastic barrel filled with ice and soft drinks. Jeff fished out two sodas, popped the tabs, and handed me one. "So how did your ESL meeting go?" he asked. "Did you decide to sign up?"

I was flattered that he remembered, but then he seemed to recall a lot of the things I said to him. "Yeah," I replied. "It sounds as if it will be hard work, but they only asked us to sign up for one afternoon a week, so it shouldn't be too bad."

"I think it's really nice that you're doing it," Jeff said. "All that work takes a special kind of person."

The compliment made me feel warm all over. "Thanks," I said. "Actually, hosting a foreign exchange student gave me the idea. I mean, Karin speaks English really well, but it's still her second language, and you wouldn't believe how many misunderstandings come up."

Jeff nodded. "I guess that never occurred to me. It must be interesting, having Karin live with you."

"Mostly it's great," I said. "I'm an only child, so I've always wanted to find out what it would be like to have a sibling around the house."

"So how is it?" Jeff raised his eyebrows.

"Really different," I told him, thinking about Karin's taking my curling iron, playing my stereo, and getting compliments on my red sweater. Here I was alone with Jeff, and all I could talk about was Karin. I was going to have to stop acting as though my new sister and I were joined with handcuffs.

"So how's the basketball team shaping up?" I asked, trying to change the subject. "Do you think we'll beat Alameda this year?"

Jeff frowned, crushing his soda can in one hand. "I think we've got it made. But some of the guys are worried about the new school rule that athletes have to keep up a C average or get benched."

"You mean, basketball players really *are* a bunch of dumb jocks?" I teased.

"Not this one," Jeff said, tapping his chest

with one finger "Believe it or not, I'm in line for an academic scholarship. One of our forwards is a little shaky, but the rest of us are doing okay. The football team has got it a lot worse. They could lose a couple of heavy hitters this season, even Don Bradley."

I was astonished to hear that Don, Greeley's star quarterback, had such low grades. Football is a complicated game, and it was hard to think of Don Bradley as a dumb jock. "I thought quarterbacks had to be pretty smart," I said.

Jeff shrugged. "Don's been in a few of my classes, and he's no dummy, that's for sure. I guess he's just more interested in football than academics. A lot of athletes are like that."

"So what makes you different?" I asked. Jeff Shafer was turning out to be every bit as special as I'd imagined. He was great looking, an excellent student *and* athlete, and he was the best partner with whom I'd ever danced. And on top of all that, he was sensitive and modest.

In fact, he was so modest that my question seemed to embarrass him a little. He hunched his shoulders and said, "I'm not sure I'm all that different."

He glanced around the room and waved at

someone. I looked over to see Karin coming toward us.

"Where's David?" Jeff asked her. "Last time I saw him, he looked as if he wasn't planning to let you get away."

Karin laughed. "He is a very nice boy, but I hope he has no plans about me. I already have a boyfriend." She looked a little sad.

When Karin first told me about Niels, my only thought had been how lucky I was not to have to compete with her for boys. Now I started thinking how lonely she probably was without him. "You must really miss Niels at times like this," I said. "Especially since you're not dating anyone else."

"A party would be much more fun for me if he were here," Karin said. "But having so many nice kids around helps to make up for it."

Jeff gave her a sympathetic smile. "If you ever want a date that you don't have to get serious about, I could fix something up for you."

"Thanks," Karin said, "but I am afraid I would feel—how do you say, not loyal to Niels." Suddenly she rolled her eyes to the ceiling. "Here is David again. I think I must tell him of Niels."

"Yeah," Jeff said. "Maybe you'd better. I think he's got serious designs on you."

David grinned at Jeff and me, then grabbed Karin by both hands and towed her toward the dance floor. A slow song was starting, and Jeff gave me a questioning look. "Slow dancing isn't my strong point," I told him, "but I have a feeling I could dance to anything with you."

"Flattery will get you everywhere," Jeff said.

I laughed as he put his arm around my waist, and everything around us started to fade again. Then he pulled me closer. I let my forehead rest on Jeff's shoulder, enjoying the feel of his arms around me and the clean, fresh way he smelled. He was holding me so close that I could hear his heart beating.

I closed my eyes, wondering if Jeff felt as happy as I did. We were dancing so slowly that our feet barely moved, but just as before, we were in perfect time with each other. Near the end of the song, we stopped moving our feet altogether and stayed where we were, holding each other. I felt as if I'd been hypnotized. Finally, Jeff broke my trance by giving me a quick squeeze.

Almost immediately, another song came on, and then we danced fast to one song after another. Every now and then, someone passed by us and said good night, but Jeff and I just waved and kept dancing. Eventually, we were so exhausted we had to stop.

By then, all but a dozen kids had left the party. Jeff looked around in surprise. "Where did everyone go?"

He looked so bewildered that I couldn't help laughing. "Didn't you hear them saying good-bye? I guess I'd better get going, too. Karin is probably bored to death waiting for me."

"What?" Jeff said, pretending to be indignant. "Nobody gets bored at my parties."

"Oh, yeah? Well, what about *after* your parties? I'd say this one is history."

"Okay, if that's how you want it to be, I'll walk you to your car." He put on a hurt expression, then suddenly grinned. "It's been fun. I'm really glad you came."

"Me, too," I said, wishing the party could have gone on forever.

We found Karin talking to some other kids near the foot of the stairs. "It is about time," she said. "I was afraid you would dance all night."

Jeff and I just smiled at each other. A few minutes later, the three of us walked out to the car. I climbed in behind the steering wheel and turned to say good night to Jeff. He was leaning his elbows in the open window, just as he had the day we met—except this time he was wearing a very different expression.

The look on my face must have been different, too, because Jeff leaned toward me and kissed me lightly on the mouth. His lips were smooth and warm and tasted a little like orange soda, but at the moment I wasn't really aware of that. I only knew that Jeff Shafer was kissing me, and my heart was pounding so hard I was afraid he could hear it.

Chapter Five

"And so," Karin said, winding up her report to our history class, "although the Vikings raided the coasts of Europe more than one thousand years ago, and Norway is now a modern country with industry and trade much as you have in America, the Viking tradition has given us our great merchant shipping fleet, for which my country is famous."

She looked around at the class, a bit hesitantly, and then someone behind me started clapping. I joined in, and soon we were all applauding.

Just as we were quieting down, the bell rang, and school was over. Karin and I always walked home together after class, so I waited outside the door for her. "Your report was great," I said when she came out. "You really made everything come alive with all the details."

Karin looked a little embarrassed. "It was not so much," she said. "I told only what we learn in Norway's schools."

I shook my head and smiled at her. Karin seemed to do everything perfectly, without even having to try. But by now I was so used to her instant successes that I hardly resented her anymore.

Karin stopped at her locker, and I went on to mine, which was at the other end of the hall. When I got there, I saw Jeff leaning casually against the wall. I was so surprised that I almost stopped breathing. After the night he'd kissed me, I expected him to ask me out. We saw each other almost every day at school, and he always acted as if he liked me. But more than a week and a half had gone by since the party, and Jeff still hadn't asked me for a date.

Now I didn't know what to think, so I started fumbling with my locker combination and said, "Hi. Waiting for someone?"

"Yep. You. I was hoping I'd catch you here."

"Well, here I am," I said, trying to sound nonchalant.

Jeff straightened up and reached over to hold my books while I opened my locker. "Listen," he said, "you'll think this is dumb, but would you like to go to Disneyland this Saturday? We'd be going with a couple of guys from the team and their girlfriends."

Now that I'd almost given up on him, Jeff was finally asking me out! I was so excited I nearly shouted. "Sure! It sounds like fun."

Jeff went on talking as though he hadn't heard me. "I know you've probably been there a million times, but . . ."

"I could never get tired of Disneyland," I said quickly. "It's one of my favorite places." I would have gone almost anywhere with Jeff, but I was telling the truth about Disneyland. Some people thought it was only for little kids, but I never got enough of the roller coaster or the ride through the pirate cave.

But Jeff still didn't seem to believe me. "You're kidding!"

"No, I'm not," I said, taking back my books. "What time will we go?"

Jeff suddenly looked blank. "I'm not sure yet. I'll find out and tell you tomorrow, okay?"

"Great," I said. Just then, Karin came up.

"What is great?" she asked. "Am I missing something?"

"Not yet," Jeff said. "Vicki and I were just making plans to go to Disneyland this weekend." He gave me a questioning look, and before I knew what was happening, he'd turned back to Karin. "Hey, you should definitely see Disneyland while you're here. Why don't you come along?"

I could hardly believe my ears. This was our first real date, and Jeff was inviting Karin to go with us! I crossed my fingers, hoping she would refuse.

"Disneyland is the Mickey Mouse Club?" she asked.

Jeff laughed. "Well, it's a lot more than that. There are rides, shows, music, exhibits— even shops and food."

Karin nodded. "I think, then, that I must see it."

"Good," Jeff said. "Listen, can I give you two a ride home?"

I started to say "sure," but then I remembered I had my first English-as-a-second-language tutoring session that afternoon. "What time is it?" I asked.

Jeff glanced at his watch. "Three forty-five."

"I have ESL today," I said reluctantly. "It almost slipped my mind. I'm tutoring a freshman whose family just moved here from Mexico. I've got to get going, or I'll be late."

"Okay," Jeff said. "I'll drop Karin off, and I'll talk to you tomorrow."

"All right. See you." I was so confused that I wasn't sure whether I should laugh or cry. What I really wanted to do was scream, I decided. I'd waited so long for Jeff Shafer to ask me out, and now that he finally had, Karin was coming along, too. And if that wasn't bad enough, she was riding home with Jeff while I hung around at school teaching ESL.

It wasn't fair, I thought as I walked down the hall. It seemed that whenever I started feeling good about Karin, something else would go wrong. And whatever went wrong always seemed to include Jeff. Now, at that very moment, Karin was alone with him because I had decided to be a tutor. It was all pretty ironic. If it hadn't been for Karin, I probably wouldn't have signed up for ESL to begin with.

That night at dinner, I was still annoyed about Karin and Jeff. Unfortunately, my dad was in one of his cheerful moods.

"Well," he said brightly, looking from me to Karin. "How are things going at Greeley High School?"

That was his idea of a good conversation starter. My dad was very intelligent and fairly good-looking in his own way. He had a lot of other nice qualities, too, but he wasn't very skillful at small talk.

"Fine," I said, trying to help him along. "Karin gave a report on Vikings today in history. The class practically gave her a standing ovation."

"Really?" he said, turning to Karin. "You must be a very talented girl."

Karin blushed and speared a piece of broccoli with her fork. "I think I am not so talented," she said. "It is only that Americans are so friendly and enthusiastic."

"I'm sure you deserved some of the credit," my mom said.

"Perhaps a little," Karin said. "But mostly it is that kids here have given me such a warm welcome. Vicki's friend, Jeff, I think, makes a special effort to—include me. Do you say this? Today he has given me a ride home, and Saturday we will all go together to Disneyland."

I'd told my mom that I was interested in Jeff. She nodded and gave me an approving smile. "He sounds like a nice boy."

That was too much. Jeff *was* a nice boy, but "including Karin" wasn't what made me think so. "Yeah," I replied sarcastically. "He's a real peach."

Suddenly everyone was staring at me. Karin had that confused look on her face that she always got when she didn't understand something I'd said. My mom's expression said she understood *what* I'd said, but not *why*.

Dad didn't seem to have any idea of what was going on at all. "It sounds as though you're not as pleased with him as Karin is, Vicki," he said.

I looked down at the table, wishing I'd kept my mouth shut. Suddenly the food started swimming around my plate. I didn't realize right away that that was because I had tears in my eyes. "I'm sorry I made that remark," I said. "I guess I just need some time to myself. May I be excused?"

My dad nodded helplessly, and I got up from my chair and went to my room. A little while later, my mom knocked, then peeked in the door. "It's okay," I said. "You can come in."

I was sitting in one corner of my daybed with my back propped against the pillows. She sat down cross-legged at the other end of the bed. For some reason I was always surprised to see her do that. But my mom was an unusual person in lots of ways. With her great blond hair, incredible cheekbones, and thick, dark eyelashes, she could have looked like a soap opera star if she wanted to, but instead she usually dressed in baggy pants and used hardly any makeup.

That night she wasn't even wearing lipstick, and somehow that made her seem very relaxed and easy to talk to. I told her about Jeff inviting me to Disneyland, and then inviting Karin, too.

"I don't see why you're so upset about that," Mom said. "I thought you and Karin really liked each other."

"We do like each other," I said. "Karin is terrific, but do I have to share *everything* with her? Just once, I'd like to be alone with Jeff."

My mom thought for a minute. "I see what you mean," she said at last. "But what about Jeff? Are you sure *he* wants to be alone with *you*?"

That really knocked me over. "Well, I think so. I mean, I know he likes me. We danced together all evening at his party. He even kissed me good night."

Telling her that Jeff had kissed me was embarrassing, but she just shrugged. "Some boys just need more time. If you ask me, it's Jeff—not Karin—who's keeping you two from being alone. There'll be other kids going along to Disneyland anyway. Why shouldn't Karin go, too?"

I was getting more confused by the minute. "I don't know," I said. "It's just that lately, it seems as if I run into Karin everywhere I turn."

Mom looked sympathetic. "I know that having Karin here is a big adjustment for you, honey. But you knew it might be difficult sometimes before you invited her to stay with us. I think it's very nice of Jeff to help you look out for her."

It had never occurred to me that Jeff was helping with Karin. Somehow, I couldn't quite believe that was true. "Maybe," I said slowly, "but I don't think she really needs anyone to watch out for her. The kids at school are crazy about her. Why can't she go out with some of *them* now and then?"

"Maybe they haven't asked her," my mom said. "After all, she's only been here a few weeks. Can't you give her a little more time?"

I didn't know what other choice I had, so I agreed. Nothing was going as I'd expected, but I had to admit that that was partly my fault. I'd only imagined all the fun things Karin and I would do together—like shopping, walking to school, and double-dating.

The part I *hadn't* thought about was that my whole life would be turned upside down. I'd been used to being alone, and now I had to share absolutely everything with Karin—including Jeff Shafer.

But maybe my mom was right, I decided at last. Jeff might be taking an interest in Karin mostly to help me out. The idea that he was doing something like that for *me* gave the situation a whole new slant. Just thinking about it made me feel warm all over.

Chapter Six

Jeff was supposed to pick us up on Saturday morning around eleven o'clock. The day was bright and sunny, with a mild autumn breeze—perfect weather for a trip to Disneyland.

I dressed carefully in white jeans and a purple T-shirt, then tried out a few different ways of pulling back my hair. I had just decided on a braid when my telephone rang. I grabbed it on the second ring, thinking it would be Jeff calling about some last-minute detail. Instead, the person on the other end of the line turned out to be Don Bradley.

"Hey, Vicki," he said. "Coach LaRue gave me your number. Listen, you know that new rule about athletes having to keep a C average?"

"Yes," I replied, wondering what he was getting at. "I heard some of the football players were put on academic probation."

"Man, that really bums me out," Don said. "Coach says I talk so bad I ought to be in ESL. He's benching me until I get my act together."

"He can't do that!" I cried instantly. "The team will never beat Alameda High without you!"

"That's what I told the coach, you know? So he says, like, if that's how I see it, it's up to me to do something about it. I heard you were tutoring, so can you help me out?"

"What?" I still didn't understand what he was talking about, but then things suddenly started falling into place. "You mean tutor you in English?"

"Yeah," Don said. "Like help me make my grades."

"Oh," I said. "I don't know."

Don let out a frustrated sigh. "Oh, man, I am really desperate. I'll do *anything*, Vicki. Homework, no messing around, anything you say. Just save my neck, all right?"

I hesitated. I owed it to Greeley to help keep Don on the playing field, but at the same time, I couldn't help thinking about Karin with Jeff the first time I'd had a tutoring session. But if Jeff saw me spending a lot of time with Greeley's star quarterback, maybe he would feel a little jealous of me for a change.

"Okay," I agreed at last. "When do you want to start?"

Don let out a loud whoop. "The first available minute. Vicki, if you can bail me out of this, I promise you I'll never forget it."

He sounded so grateful that I nearly blushed. "Okay," I said. "Let's get together after school on Tuesday."

As I hung up the phone, I wondered what I was getting myself into. Don's English was obviously far from perfect, and just getting him up to normal would take hours of work. But I'd already said I would do it, so there was no point in worrying about it.

I looked in the mirror and decided to leave my hair loose instead of pulling it back. I'd just put away my hairbrush when Jeff arrived to pick us up.

Jeff was driving his mother's station wagon, but it was already so full of people that we could barely squeeze in. Karin climbed into the back with two guys and another girl. Jeff held open the driver's door for me, and I slid past the steering wheel to sit between him and another boy.

"Guess what?" I said as Jeff backed the car out of my driveway. "Don Bradley just called me. He's off the team until he gets his grades up in English."

Before I could say anything more, everyone in the car started groaning. "Man, Alameda's going to walk all over our team if we don't have our star player," the boy next to me said. "Bradley had better find some way to pull himself together."

"He asked me to tutor him," I said. "And I said yes."

I knew I'd made the right decision when everyone burst out cheering. Jeff patted my knee and said, "Good move, Vicki." He didn't seem at all jealous, but right then it didn't matter. His smile was so approving that I felt as if I were floating on air.

I was still feeling giddy awhile later when Jeff and I got in line for a ride called Pirates of the Caribbean. As soon as we'd walked through the gate to Disneyland, everyone wanted to do something different, so after a while, I suggested that we split up and meet later. Of course, I was really hoping for a chance to be alone with Jeff.

Jeff and I were together for more than an hour; we'd gone on the Matterhorn roller coaster twice. My stomach always did flip-flops when our car reached the top of the mountain, but that day it had done double flips. That was partly because we were riding in the front car and partly because Jeff put his arm around me whenever we roared into a downhill curve.

Now I was looking forward to the romantic boat ride through the dark pirate cave. The air on the boat dock where we were waiting was damp and balmy, and soft music drifted across from a restaurant on the other side of the river.

Then we heard screams and splashing sounds, and the first boat pulled up to the dock. Jeff took my hand as we stepped aboard. A few minutes later, we were cruising down the river, surrounded by weeping willows and a starry evening sky.

"The first part of this ride is so romantic," I said, snuggling against Jeff's shoulder. "I always feel like I'm actually in the Old South."

Jeff put his arm around me and frowned. "Pardon me, ma'am, but I thought this really *was* the Old South. I think I'll ask for my money back."

I looked up into his eyes and laughed. "No

way. This is one of my favorite rides, so you may as well settle down and enjoy it."

"Oh, all right," Jeff said. "But I want you to know I wouldn't do this with just anyone."

"You'd better not!" My cheeks started flaming as soon as the words were out. Here I was acting as if I owned him, and we hadn't even been on a real date yet!

Jeff gave me a long look, then grinned and shook his head. I was going to explain that I'd only been teasing, but Jeff didn't give me a chance. "That's what I like," he said. "A girl who says exactly what's on her mind."

Suddenly the boat lurched around a corner, plunging us into pitch darkness. Jeff pulled me closer and gently kissed me on the cheek. His lips were soft and warm, and their touch left a glow on my skin that I could feel even after they were gone. Maybe I hadn't put my foot in my mouth after all, I decided, and then I screamed as our boat shot downhill into the rapids. The boat bounced around crazily, and Jeff and I held on to each other tightly until the rapids were past and the ride smoothed out.

The pirate den appeared on our right, and we could see the pirates singing and counting their money. The scene was kid stuff, but it was so silly and cheerful that it always made me want to giggle. I glanced at Jeff. I could barely see him in the dark, but I sensed him turning toward me at the same moment, and we laughed together.

It's just like when we danced, I thought. *We're really in sync with each other.*

The boat wound through the cave for a while longer, and then the evening sky appeared in the distance. Before I knew it, we were stepping back onto the dock.

"That was fun," Jeff said. "I guess there are some things I'll never outgrow."

I grinned. "Me either," I said. "What do you want to do next?"

Jeff thought for a minute, then glanced at his digital watch. "I'd like to check out the space exhibit, but I'm not sure we have time. We're supposed to meet everyone at the carousel in half an hour."

At his reminder of Karin and the others, I almost groaned aloud. "Already?" I said. Jeff got a funny look on his face, and I wondered if I'd said something wrong again. "I mean, there must be something we can do for half an hour," I added quickly, "instead of just waiting around."

"Yeah," Jeff said. "We could eat three or four frozen bananas."

I made a face. "Yuck."

"Hey, be fair," Jeff said, spinning around to look for an ice-cream stand. "You make *me* ride through the pirate cave, but when it's something *I* want to do, all you can say is 'yuck.' Whatever happened to equal rights, huh?"

"Some politician you're going to be," I said. "What do frozen bananas have to do with equal rights?" Jeff just grabbed my hand and started towing me toward a pink- and white-striped ice-cream cart.

By the time we'd finished our bananas and ice cream, it really was time to meet the others. We found them waiting for us near the carousel. Karin's face was flushed with excitement. "Your Disneyland is all you say," she exclaimed, laughing. "I have just had my photo taken with Mickey Mouse."

I looked at the picture she held toward me and smiled. Karin was gazing curiously at a giant Mickey Mouse, who stood with one arm around her shoulder, rolling his eyes comically. "That's great," I said, handing the photo to Jeff. "I'll bet you can't wait to write home about it."

"Yeah," Jeff said, "but what is good old Niels going to think when he sees you in another guy's arms?"

The idea of Niels being jealous of Mickey

Mouse made everyone laugh, but I was a little annoyed to see Jeff and Karin kidding around together again so quickly. There was nothing I could do about it, though, so I laughed along with them to hide my disappointment at not being the center of Jeff's attention.

I think Jeff picked up on my feelings, anyway, because he brought it up later. After we'd dropped off everyone else and pulled up to my house, Karin went inside and left Jeff and me standing in the driveway beside the car. "Thanks for inviting me," I said. "I had a wonderful time."

"Me, too," Jeff said. "I was afraid you'd think going to Disneyland was dumb."

"I thought guys like you weren't afraid of anything," I said, teasing him.

"Everyone's afraid of something," he replied, taking my hand. He stared down at my fingers, folding them in and out from my palm and looking thoughtful. After a minute, he shrugged and smiled shyly. "I guess I'm really afraid of looking stupid." Suddenly he looked up and grinned. "You know, dumb jocks and all that."

I laughed. "That's ridiculous. Anyway, I'm glad you got up the nerve to ask me." I paused. "Maybe you and I could go to a movie or something sometime. I mean, without Karin and everyone."

Jeff stopped playing with my fingers and looked at me curiously. "Without Karin, huh? I had the feeling you were trying to ditch her today. What's going on?"

I hesitated. Jeff had just said that everyone was afraid of something. What I was scared of right then was what Jeff would think if he knew how I really felt about Karin. But I also felt that he wanted me to tell him the truth. He could probably see right through me anyway, so there was no point in pretending.

"It's just that I never realized Karin was going to be doing *everything* with me," I said finally. "I guess I'm not used to that." I shrugged and glanced away. "My mother thinks I'm being selfish. You probably think so, too."

Jeff looked thoughtful again, then bent down and kissed the tip of my nose. "Maybe a little," he said. "But I can sort of understand why you feel that way, too."

"You can?" I asked hopefully.

Jeff nodded, and then his face broke into that mischievous smile. "Yeah. Listen, I wouldn't mind spending some time alone with you, either. Would you like to go to a movie next Saturday?"

Would I? I was totally ecstatic, but all I could manage to say was, "Yeah. That'd be great."

"Okay," Jeff said. "We'll check out what's playing and decide later." He grinned again. "But don't be surprised when you see how boring I can be alone for a whole evening."

"Okay," I agreed. Somehow I didn't think that would be a problem.

Chapter Seven

The next few days went by about as fast as a herd of turtles racing a team of snails. Now that Jeff and I had finally scheduled a real date, I thought Saturday would never come.

I saw Jeff around school a few times on Monday, and he ate lunch with Karin and me and the rest of our crowd. After school, he had a meeting with the basketball team, so Karin and I walked home together.

Tuesday, I had my first tutoring session with Don Bradley. I said good-bye to Karin outside our last class, wondering whether she'd walk home alone or get a ride with Jeff. I decided it would be better not to think about it.

Don was already waiting for me on the front steps. "Man, am I glad to see you," he said, his wide face brightening instantly. "What do you say we head over to Guido's?"

I narrowed my eyes at him. "Not a chance, Don. We work in an ESL classroom or nowhere."

Don looked bewildered. "Hey, what's to keep us from munching a pizza while we hit the books?"

He sounded as though he had one hand in the cookie jar and was still hoping I wouldn't catch him. "Your buddies," I said firmly. "The jukebox. Girls."

He shrugged, looking so trapped that I couldn't help smiling. Don was as tall as Jeff and twice as wide. He had short blond hair, icy blue eyes, and a broad face with a short, square nose. He looked tough, but I was beginning to see that he was a marshmallow at heart.

"By the way, Don," I said, trying to look stern. "Where are your books?"

He looked down at his empty hands. "Hey, give me a break, Vicki. This is only our first rally. How was I supposed to know what books to bring?"

I just shook my head. Finally he gave me a guilty grin. "Jeez, Kenyon, you are one tough cookie. Have you ever thought about going out for linebacker?"

I had a feeling Don and I were going to get along fine. "You must be a good quarterback," I said. "You always push for the last inch, don't you?"

"Yeah," he admitted, "but when somebody blows the whistle on me, I'm usually a good sport."

"We'd better start with basic grammar," I said, starting to walk toward an ESL classroom. "Fortunately, I just happen to have *my* book."

Don grinned and raised his hands in surrender. "Okay, teach. I'm all yours."

He meant it, too. I drilled him on punctuation for a long time, and he didn't complain once. It was nearly five o'clock when we finally agreed to quit. "This is the most fun I've had since we got pulverized by Alameda," Don joked. "What are you doing tomorrow?"

I grimaced. Thursday I'd have my regular ESL session, and I hated staying late on Fridays. That left Wednesday or the following week. "How about next Tuesday?" I asked.

Don's face crumpled like an accordion. For a second, I almost thought he was going to cry. "Listen," he said, "here's the deal. Willie Farrow and me, we're on probation—"

"Willie Farrow and I," I corrected.

Don looked confused. "Willie and you what? You tutoring him, too?"

At first, I was sure he was teasing, but then I saw his serious expression, and I swallowed my giggle. "No," I said. "I meant you should say 'Willie and I.' Because it's the subject of the sentence. You say 'Willie and me' when it's the object."

Watching Don's face was like looking at a slide show. It went from blank to annoyed and then finally, to understanding. "Yeah, okay," he said. "Anyway, Willie and I can't play officially, but we go out for practice. They're making us take this test in a couple of weeks, and if we don't pass, we're off the team. Man, do you know what that means? They'll get another quarterback, and I'm into the dumper for good."

Don had to be the most open boy I'd ever met. His emotions were written all over his face. Now his dismay was so obvious that my heart went out to him. "Okay, listen," I said. "We're going to need every minute we can get. I'm free Monday through Wednesday, and maybe we could work some weekends, if we have to."

Don's expression brightened as if I'd just flipped on a light switch. "All right! You're

A-okay, after all. Listen, how you gettin' home? I could drop you off."

"Sure," I said. "That would be great."

As we walked to his car, I couldn't help noticing how relaxed I felt with Don. We'd only spent a couple of hours together, but I was already beginning to like him. Not in a romantic way, of course. Don wasn't the kind of guy I'd ever dream about. I just had a feeling we might end up being buddies.

"Thanks for the ride," I said, as we pulled up to my house. "See you tomorrow."

Don grinned. "You can bet your life on it, man. And next time, I'll bring my own grammar book."

"Great," I said. "And would you mind not calling me 'man'? My name is Vicki."

"Sorry," Don replied, looking embarrassed. "I can handle that." His expression turned serious. "Oh, man, Vicki, *two lousy weeks*! How's a dumb cluck like me gonna learn three years of grammar in two weeks?"

He sounded desperate, but the way he'd worked in my name after "oh, man" was pretty comical. I almost wanted to hug him, but instead, I patted his arm. "You're not a dumb cluck," I said firmly. "You're a smart quarterback, and you're going to make it through this test. Inch by inch."

Don's face brightened again. "It's like moving the ball to the goalpost, huh?"

"Yeah," I replied, wondering why I hadn't thought of that image myself. "Only this time, the goal is the test. See you tomorrow, okay?"

I hopped out of the car and walked into the house, thinking about what Don had just said. Maybe if I could make English more like football, Don would pick it up faster.

But I didn't know enough about football to take that idea any further. Jeff might be able to help me, though—and besides, it would give me a good excuse to call him.

I headed for my room, trying to remember Jeff's number, but when I walked in, Karin was already there, using my phone. She was curled up on one corner of the daybed, looking very small and almost childlike. Somehow, the scene reminded me of the day we'd picked her up at the airport.

"It makes me a little nervous, coming to such a big city," Karin had said. Her words had astonished me, considering how sophisticated she looked. *"Don't worry,"* I had said, *"you'll have me to help you."*

The same protective feeling came over me again. She glanced up at me, raising her eyebrows and pointing at the phone as if to ask if I wanted to use it. I quickly shook my head and dropped my books on one of the wicker chairs. I could talk to Jeff later, I decided, and I headed for the kitchen to see if my parents needed help making dinner.

My mom was on her hands and knees, searching for something in the bottom cupboard. When I walked in, she looked at me over her shoulder. "How did the tutoring go?"

"Okay. Don Bradley's a really nice guy."

She stood up and brushed off her hands on her jeans. The way she'd pulled back her hair in a ponytail made her look like a kid. "I thought you were stuck on Jeff," she said, her eyes widening.

"Don is just a friend," I explained. "I'm really excited about going out with Jeff this weekend. The only thing is," I went on, "I feel a little guilty about Karin. Between tutoring Don and tutoring my ESL student, I'll be busy Monday through Thursday. Plus I'll be dating Jeff."

My mom looked sympathetic. "I think you're overworking the problem, honey. First you were worried about spending too much time with Karin, and now you're afraid of not spending enough."

"I know," I said. "But I *am* responsible for her. I mean, I can't just leave her completely alone."

"Hmmm," Mom said thoughtfully, sticking her hands in her hip pockets. "Why don't you ask one of your friends to invite Karin somewhere Saturday night? I bet Nancy wouldn't mind taking her to a movie or something. Unless she had a date with Gary, that is."

"You're a genius!" I said, hugging her. "I think Gary's going to San Diego this weekend, and he and Nancy aren't a steady couple anymore, anyway. I'll talk to her tomorrow."

By the time the weekend finally came, all my problems seemed to be solved. Wednesday at lunch, Jeff had helped me work out a study plan for Don. We divided the material into "downs" we had to make in order to score. A down was ten yards, a touchdown was a hundred yards, and we had ten days to get there.

That same afternoon, I told Don about the plan. Looking at it as if it were a football game, he began to see his English test as a challenge. "So I've gotta make ten yards a day," he said. "Man, we'd better go for some extra yards—just in case we get hit with a last-minute turnaround."

Before that day's session was over, Don had promised to be at the forty-yard line by Monday. Somehow, I felt certain he could do it. Tutoring him was turning out to be fun, and it was also improving my relationship with Karin. Now that we were seeing less of each other, the time we did spend together seemed more special.

Nancy had invited Karin to go to a movie Saturday night, and that Saturday afternoon, the three of us went shopping together. Afterward, we went to my house and listened to records for a while. Nancy and Karin were going to the first show, so they were already gone by the time Jeff came to pick me up.

Jeff arrived at seven-thirty, wearing baggy tan slacks and a black jersey under a tan camp shirt. He still had a deep summer tan, and he looked so gorgeous that I just stood there in the doorway, staring at him and grinning like an idiot.

"Excuse me," he said, after a minute. "I was looking for Vicki Kenyon."

"Sorry," I said, laughing. "You look great in that outfit."

"Thanks," he said. "You're looking pretty good yourself. Too bad I can't stick around, but I've got this date, you know? Well, it was nice meeting you." He turned around as if he were about to leave.

"Come back here!" I ordered, grabbing him by the sleeve and pulling him back through the door.

Jeff frowned, then grabbed me by the shoulders and kissed me hard. "Mmm," he said, licking his lips. "Maybe I've got the right house, after all."

"You'd better believe it," I replied, "but just to make sure . . ."

I stood on my toes and kissed Jeff back. He licked his lips again, pretending he still wasn't certain. "It's coming back to me," he said.

I laughed. "At this rate, the movie will be over before we even get to the theater. Come on." I took Jeff's hand and led him into the living room to meet my parents. Finally we were riding down the freeway in his black RX 7.

I settled back in the bucket seat. It was this car that had brought Jeff and me together, and it felt incredibly right for me to be riding in it. I stole a glance at Jeff. I liked the way he looked, thought, danced, drove, and especially the way he kissed. In fact, I couldn't think of anything I *didn't* like about him, except that he made it so hard to spend time alone with him.

Even Jeff's taste in movies was excellent, I soon learned. Since there was nothing I particularly wanted to see, I'd left the choice up to him. The film he picked was one I would probably never have chosen. It was about four kids and was set in the 1950s.

The theater was crowded, and some of the kids near us were horsing around. But Jeff and I got so caught up in the movie that we hardly noticed. At first, the film was funny, and not especially exciting. In the second half, though, the suspense gradually mounted, and then I got so tense that I grabbed Jeff's hand without even realizing what I was doing. He put his arm around me, and we snuggled together until the movie ended.

"I can't believe how kids back then were so much like kids today," I said, as we walked out of the theater and into the mall. "I mean, they looked different, but the things they thought about were the same."

"Yeah," Jeff said. "But the world has changed a lot. Did you see that old gas station? And how everyone in town seemed to know one another?"

"You're right," I agreed. "Can you imagine knowing everyone in Los Angeles? Or even in Anaheim, for that matter. You'd be so busy saying 'how are you' that you wouldn't have time for anything else."

Jeff laughed. "So much for the good old days. Would you rather go for ice cream or pizza?"

I shrugged. "Either's okay. Why don't we walk down the mall and decide on the way? Maybe we'll see something we can't resist."

Jeff put his arm around my waist. "In that case, we can stop right here. I already see something I can't resist."

"What?" I turned to see what he was talking about before I realized what he'd meant. My insides began to flutter like crazy. "The feeling is definitely mutual," I said, looking up into his eyes. I laughed nervously. "What were you thinking?" I asked.

"Huh-uh," Jeff said. "You first."

I shrugged. "I just laughed because I was happy. And because we were both looking so serious. Okay, now you."

"Me, too," he said. "It made me think of the day you almost ran into me at the car wash. I thought you were going to bite my head off."

"Me!" I exclaimed. "When you came over to my car, you looked as if you wanted to have me arrested!"

Jeff hunched his head into his shoulders like King Kong or the Incredible Hulk. "Ve haf vays of dealing with vomen drivers," he said.

I giggled.

"Darn," Jeff said. "I can't shock you at all. Hey," he said suddenly. "Let's go to McNulty's. We can get a hot fudge sundae and play the pinball machines."

"Great," I said.

We walked into the brightly lit restaurant and checked out the crowd. A soda fountain with stools covered one wall, and along the other were pinball machines and computer games. The rest of the room was filled with big round booths, which were now jammed with kids.

Jeff and I walked down the aisle, holding hands and searching for an empty booth. "Vicki! Jeff!" someone yelled. I turned around to see Karin waving over the back of a booth, where she was sitting with Nancy and a girl from Greeley named Kim.

My heart sank. I'd been trying for weeks to get an evening alone with Jeff. I'd spent the whole afternoon with Karin and arranged for Nancy to take her out that night. Now, just when everything was going perfectly, the first person I'd run into was Karin.

Fortunately, she had plenty of company, so I waved and went on looking for a private booth. But Jeff had a different idea. As soon as he saw Karin, he let go of my hand and started back down the aisle. "Hey! Nancy, Karin, it's nice to see you. Hi, Kim."

"Hi," the three of them chorused.

Karin smiled warmly. "What luck that we ran into you," she said, sliding over to make room for us. The next thing I knew, I was sitting between her and Jeff. A few minutes later, even more kids arrived and started crowding in with us.

"Hey, Vicki," someone called. "What's the latest on Don Bradley? Is he going to make his grades?"

I shrugged and forced myself to smile. "I think there's a good chance."

"He'd better," another boy said. "The game with Alameda is less than three weeks away."

Everyone was laughing and talking, but my heart wasn't in the conversation. I began to realize that earlier in the evening Jeff had been openly affectionate toward me. But now that we were with Karin and the others, he was treating me like a buddy. It seemed as if he could only show his feelings for me when we were alone together.

A waitress came to our table, and we ordered hot fudge sundaes. "Hey," I finally said to Jeff, "didn't you challenge me to a game of pinball?"

Jeff looked blank, but Karin said, "Pinball? What is this pinball you talk about?"

Of course, Jeff immediately started explaining the game to her. I sighed, wishing she would just keep her mouth shut. I fumed silently as Jeff led Karin to one of the machines for a demonstration. I barely said a word when they rejoined us after the sundaes arrived.

"How come you were so quiet tonight?" Jeff asked as we walked back to his car at the end of the evening.

I shrugged. "Maybe I didn't have anything to say."

"Oh, sure," Jeff said, threading his fingers through mine and swinging our hands. "Vicki Kenyon at a loss for words."

I laughed halfheartedly. "It can happen to anyone," I said. "Especially when you can hardly get a word in edgewise."

Jeff looked at me sharply. "Don't tell me you're down on Karin again."

"I'm not exactly *down* on her," I said. "I just thought you and I were going to spend some time alone together."

We reached the car, and I waited while Jeff unlocked the door for me. "Don't you think you're being a little unfair?" he asked, climbing into the driver's seat. "It's not Karin's fault that we happened to turn up at the same place."

"Oh, sure," I said. "And I guess it's not her fault that we had to sit with her, either."

Jeff glanced at me and started the car. "Actually, it was my fault. I thought it would be fun."

That was the last straw. Ever since the moment we'd sat down with Karin, I had been growing more annoyed by the minute. By that time I was so furious that my face felt like it was on fire. "Well, *I* didn't think it would be fun. I suppose that never occurred to you."

"Then why didn't you just say so?" Jeff replied calmly, keeping his eyes on the road.

Why *hadn't* I said something? His question seemed so reasonable that I stared at him in confusion. "Maybe I was afraid to admit the truth," I said.

"I don't blame you," Jeff said. "Sometimes the truth is really embarrassing."

He was totally right about that, but he didn't have to rub it in. "Thanks," I said, fighting back tears.

"Hey." Jeff stopped the car in front of my house and pulled me into his arms. "Vicki, I was only teasing. Trying to lighten things up, you know?"

I pulled away and glared at him. "Look," he said, "I'm embarrassed about this, too. I'm sorry I blew it, but I couldn't read your mind."

"Okay," I said. "But what if I *had* said what I was really thinking? You already admitted that you wanted to sit with those guys."

"Well, yeah. I like having lots of people

around. But this was our first date, sort of, so maybe I was out of line."

I had stopped being really mad the instant Jeff had started apologizing. Now he sounded so sincere that I smiled. Jeff grinned mischievously and put his hands on my shoulders. "Anyway," he said, "I warned you what a bore I could be when you got me alone for an evening."

After a moment I put my arms around Jeff's neck and leaned my head on his shoulder. "This is crazy," I said softly. "Our first date, and we end up fighting."

"Yeah," Jeff murmured, nuzzling his chin against my cheek. "But at least we have an excuse to kiss and make up."

"Who needs an excuse?" I murmured, closing my eyes and turning my face up to his.

Chapter Eight

Don Bradley's English test was scheduled for a Thursday. When we'd started working together, I had thought that it would be impossible to cover all the material in time. But by the day before the exam, I'd changed my mind.

Since Jeff and I had worked out his unique study plan, Don had been plowing through the material like it was Alameda High's defensive line. He now had a fair grasp of basic grammar, used commas instead of dashes, and could write a paragraph that made sense. Even more incredible, his speech had improved so much that everyone in school was teasing him about it.

But Don's spelling was still impossible. We would have to work on that all afternoon, I decided, glancing at the clock on the wall of my history classroom. A few seconds later, the bell rang, and everyone made a mad dash for the door.

Karin and I walked out of class together, and Jeff and Nancy came up to us as soon as we reached the hall. "Hey," Nancy said, "I'm meeting Gary at Guido's in half an hour. Why don't you all stop by and join us?"

"Don't tempt me," I said. "I've got a spelling date with Don Bradley. Tomorrow's the big day."

"You mean it's time for that exam already?" said Nancy. "I sure hope he makes it."

"Me, too," said Jeff. "The Alameda game is a week from Saturday."

I shrugged. "I'm pretty certain he'll do okay."

"Great," Nancy said. "Listen, guys, I've got to get going. I'll keep my fingers crossed for Don."

"We all will," Karin agreed. "He will make this game something to look forward to, yes?"

"You bet," I replied. "Well, I'd better get going, too. See you all later."

Jeff and Karin said good-bye and turned to leave. Jeff had been giving Karin rides home almost every day for the past couple of weeks.

I knew it shouldn't be a big deal, but sometimes I still couldn't help feeling jealous.

I sighed and started toward my locker. *Don't be ridiculous,* I told myself. Then Jeff called my name. "Hey, Vicki," he said, as I looked back over my shoulder. "We're all going to the big game together, aren't we?"

Naturally, he was including Karin. That didn't surprise me anymore, of course, but it didn't exactly make me ecstatic, either. These days, Karin was in on everything—except tutoring Don. I glanced from her to Jeff and shrugged. "Sure, I guess."

Jeff raised his eyebrows. "Hey, what's with this 'I guess' stuff?" He walked over to me and took me by the arm, gazing down at me with a concerned expression. He led me a couple of steps away so we wouldn't be overheard. I knew that he cared about me, but somehow, that only made me sad. Sad and annoyed. As much as Jeff and I liked each other, we could never manage to see things the same way when it came to Karin.

"Nothing," I said. There was no point in going into any of that again.

"It doesn't sound like nothing," Jeff said. "Are you uptight about Karin again?"

I sighed loudly. I was tired of talking about her, but Jeff had me cornered. Besides, things weren't really going anywhere between him and me, so what did I have to lose? "Maybe," I said at last. "I guess I'm a little jealous. You see more of Karin than you do me lately."

"Vicki, you're the one who's responsible for that," Jeff said. "Since you started tutoring, neither of us sees much of you." His voice was as soft and reasonable as ever, but his eyes seemed to darken as he spoke. Was he jealous of Don, after all? I realized instantly that he wasn't.

"I'm surprised either of you noticed," I said, my voice practically dripping with sarcasm. "You seem to be doing just fine without me."

Jeff stared at me for a long moment. Finally he groaned comically, but his eyes still looked serious. "Vicki," he said, "Karin and I are friends. Don't make something out of it that isn't there."

His expression was so sincere that I felt like an idiot again for being so suspicious. "Okay," I said. "So don't make something that isn't there out of my helping Don." As soon as the words were out, I knew how stupid they sounded. *I* was the one who was jealous, not Jeff.

"I'm not," he said. "Look, we're all counting on you to keep Don in the game. I'd have to be pretty selfish to resent what you're doing for him, wouldn't I?"

I shrugged and stared down at my feet. Was Jeff trying to say that he thought *I* was selfish for resenting his friendship with Karin? In a way, it wasn't much different from what I was doing for Don. Why couldn't I just be grateful to Jeff, instead of always feeling jealous and resentful?

Suddenly, I was so confused and embarrassed that I wanted to cry. "I guess we just don't see things the same way," I told Jeff.

I kept concentrating on the floor, feeling tears rising in the corners of my eyes. When I finally managed to look up, Jeff was watching me with a tender expression on his face that told me for sure that he cared for me. So why didn't he ever ask me out?

It was true that I was busy during the week, but that didn't explain the weekends. *Maybe Jeff couldn't stand to be alone with me.* Considering the way I'd been behaving lately, I couldn't really blame him if that were the case.

At that thought, the tears I'd been fighting spilled over and ran down my cheeks. I was so embarrassed that I wanted to run away and hide. Jeff looked surprised, then reached out and took my hand. After a minute, he kissed me very gently on both cheeks, just below my eyes where the tears had fallen.

"Sorry," Jeff said softly. "Sometimes I'm just an insensitive jerk."

I shook my head and tried to smile. "You're not a jerk," I managed to say.

"Just insensitive, huh?"

"Well . . ." I said, trying to pull myself together.

"Go ahead and say it," Jeff said. "Tact isn't one of my strong points, right?"

I couldn't help laughing. "Wait a minute," I said. "That's *my* line. I'm always mouthing off before I think."

Jeff gave me another long look. "Yeah," he said at last. "But that's partly what attracted me to you. Birds of a feather, and all that. I figured maybe you could handle my act better than a lot of girls might."

Something about his last line sounded very condescending. "And what makes you think it's my job to handle your act?" I asked.

Jeff burst out laughing. I just glared at him. "What you just said is a case in point," he explained after a few seconds. "You never let me get away with being a jerk. What did you think I meant?"

I shrugged, feeling confused again. Jeff took my other hand and looked into my eyes. "All I mean is, I can be pretty thick at times," he said. "I don't always realize it, and the last girl I got serious about didn't complain until it was too late."

Jeff smiled shyly. "Listen, I know this sounds dumb, but Halloween is a week after the big game. My family always has a party out at my uncle's beach house. We could stay over after the party and have the weekend to ourselves."

I stared at him, trying to put together everything I'd just heard. *The last girl I got serious about,* Jeff had said. Did that mean that he was serious about me? And a whole weekend together at the beach!

Jeff gave another embarrassed smile and squeezed my hand. "Well, we wouldn't exactly have the weekend to ourselves," he went on. "We'd have to do a lot of corny stuff like bobbing for apples with my parents and about fifty relatives. That probably doesn't sound much better than partying with—" He broke off and glanced at Karin, who was still waiting for him a few yards down the corridor.

"You've got to be kidding!" I exclaimed. "It sounds fabulous."

"Great," Jeff said. "We'll have to figure out some costumes soon. I mean, unless you'd rather surprise me." He grinned mischievously. "Come to think of it, you've already surprised me enough. Maybe we should try working together for a change."

I laughed. "That is *definitely* okay with me," I said. "The last time we worked together may have saved Greeley's star quarterback," I added. "And I'd better get over to the ESL room before Don gives up on me."

"Okay," said Jeff. "But if that guy is in the game next week, all the credit goes to you. Just don't let it go to your head."

"Ha!" I said, starting back toward my locker. "You're just afraid you won't be able to handle *my* act."

On Friday at noon, we all sat around the cafeteria watching the door. Don had taken his exam the day before, and the results were supposed to be out any minute. When I had asked Don how it had gone, he gave me a grim smile and rolled his eyes. Now it was lunch hour, and he was still nowhere to be seen.

"I hope this isn't a bad omen," said Jeff, biting into his second sandwich.

Nancy and Karin nodded. "What do you think Don would do if he flunked?" Nancy asked.

Jeff groaned. "Don't even mention it!"

"I'm not sure what he would do," I said, glancing nervously around the room. "But what he *wouldn't* do is show up for lunch. I doubt anyone would see him around Greeley High for at least a week."

"Yeah," Jeff said. "Football sure means a lot to him. Getting kicked off the team could ruin Don. I don't think the guys who made that new rule took that fact into account."

I looked at Jeff in surprise. "You sound as if you think they shouldn't have created the rule."

Jeff shrugged. "I don't know. People are into different things, you know? The world probably wouldn't come to an end if guys like Don Bradley flunked a few classes."

"Maybe," I said, "but it doesn't seem fair to let some kids off the hook just because they're good athletes."

"That's easy for you to say," Jeff replied. "But Don probably thinks it's unfair to make grades more important than athletic ability. Sports are his life."

I glanced anxiously at the door, then started picking at my sandwich again, feeling more and more worried by the minute. All at once, a roar of cheers and applause filled the room. My heart leapt as I looked up and saw Don charging toward me, waving both fists in the air in a victory sign.

I was so excited that tears filled my eyes, and when Don arrived at our table, I jumped up and threw my arms around his neck. "We did it!" he whooped, wrapping his arms around me and whirling me off my feet. Suddenly he stopped spinning. "I passed!" he roared. "We're going to trounce Alameda! We'll kick their rears all the way to the ocean!"

When Don put me down I looked around for Jeff, blushing furiously. What would he think of all this? At last, I spotted him standing between Nancy and Gary, chanting and cheering with everyone else. Then an idiotic grin burst over my face. For the first time in weeks, I felt as though I'd really done something right. Don was back in the game, and in the process of helping him get there, I'd made a terrific new friend. And, best of all, I had a date to spend a whole weekend with Jeff Shafer at the beach.

I looked for Don and flashed the victory sign he'd given me earlier when he'd entered the cafeteria. He returned my gesture, then threw back his head and let out a wild roar. I laughed and whooped back.

Life couldn't be more wonderful than this, I thought happily.

Chapter Nine

At the Saturday night game, Alameda High never knew what hit them. Now that Greeley had Don Bradley back, they were so fired up that they came on rougher and tougher than ever.

By the end of the second quarter, the score was fourteen to zero in our favor. The Alameda team came back from halftime looking desperate. After inching the ball down the field through most of the third quarter, they finally broke Greeley's defensive line and scored just as the buzzer went off. That was Alameda's first and only touchdown. Don started firing off passes that zeroed in to his receivers like missiles with homing devices.

By the time the final buzzer had sounded, Greeley had piled up thirty-four points to Alameda's seven.

Along with everyone else in the Greeley bleachers, I cheered and screamed through the whole game. The next morning, I was so hoarse that I could hardly talk. My throat was pretty sore for the next few days, but I didn't think much about it until the following Thursday.

That morning when my clock radio came on, I had to struggle to get my eyes open. My arms and legs were stiff and achy, and my head felt so heavy that I could barely lift it off the pillow. After a minute, I stopped trying and drifted back to sleep. The next thing I knew, my mom was sitting on the edge of my bed, feeling my forehead with the back of her hand. "I think you've got a fever," she said. "How do you feel?"

I stared up at her blankly without lifting my head. The sheets felt clammy and my pajamas were damp with sweat, but I was shivering like crazy. "I'm freezing," I muttered. "I'm too cold to have a fever."

"That's how it feels sometimes when you have the flu," she said. "Your body's thermostat gets out of whack."

I groaned and burrowed deeper into the

covers. "I don't have the flu. I *can't* be sick. Jeff and I are leaving for Newport Beach Saturday morning."

Mom smiled sympathetically and stroked my hair back from my forehead. Her hand felt cool and soothing, and I closed my eyes and dozed off again. The next thing I knew, she was propping me up on the pillows and sticking a thermometer under my tongue.

A few minutes later she took out the thermometer and held it up to the light. "What does it say?" I asked anxiously. "It's normal, isn't it?"

Mom shook her head. "I'm sorry, sweetheart, but it's nearly three degrees above normal. I want you to stay home in bed today. If you're not better tomorrow, you're going to the doctor."

I started to object, then decided it was pointless. I felt so weak that I wasn't sure I could stand up long enough to get dressed. But Halloween was still two days away. If I rested today and tomorrow, I was sure to be all better by Saturday.

"Okay," I agreed. "I'll stay home from school, but I'm still going to Newport Beach for the weekend. *Nothing* is going to stop me from spending Halloween with Jeff."

"We'll see," was all Mom said. She brought

me some aspirin and orange juice, and then I fell asleep again. Sometime later, Karin came in to visit me. I couldn't figure out why she wasn't in school until I realized with a shock that it was almost four-thirty in the afternoon. I'd slept through the entire day, without even turning on the TV or stereo.

"Everyone at school sends you their best wishes to get well soon," Karin said.

"Thanks," I said, propping myself up against the pillows. As soon as I moved, I felt dizzy, but I couldn't help noticing that Karin seemed a little down. "You don't look like yourself," I said. "Is something wrong? Are you feeling sick, too?"

Karin smiled. "I am fine. It is you we are worried about. This week at Greeley High, you are as big a star as Don Bradley. Bigger even, I think, than Jeff Shafer," she added playfully.

I knew she was trying to cheer me up, but I was too miserable to laugh. Even though I'd been in bed the whole day, I felt worse than ever. I still ached all over, my head hurt and my stomach felt queasy. Even my eyeballs hurt. In fact, they were so heavy that I had to strain just to look at Karin when she spoke to me.

"Thanks for trying to cheer me up," I said,

smiling weakly. "But I don't really feel like talking right now. Would you ask my mom to get me some more aspirin?"

"Of course," Karin said, looking sympathetic. "I hope this will be only a—what do you say? Twenty-four-hour bug?"

"Me, too," I groaned, sinking back into the pillows. I had waited too long for this weekend to spend it in bed sick. Life couldn't be that unfair.

That's what I thought *then*. Later that night when Jeff called, I found out just how unfair it could be.

"Hi," Jeff said. "How's Greeley's star tutor? Couldn't take the pressure, huh?"

"Tell my mom that," I said. "She thinks I've got the flu."

Jeff groaned. "I heard," he said. "Seriously, how are you feeling?"

The aspirin had brought down my fever a little, and hearing Jeff's voice definitely raised my spirits. But my throat was still sore, and my stomach was so upset that I hadn't eaten my dinner. "Rotten," I said, wishing it weren't true. "But I'm sure it's only a twenty-four-hour bug. I'll be better tomorrow."

"I hope so," Jeff said. "I missed you at school today."

"Me, too," I said. "I'm really looking forward to Halloween. Have you got your costume ready?"

"Yeah. I'm taking your advice and going as the Greatest American Hero. Wait till you see me in red tights. Man, have I got a great pair of legs!"

I started to giggle, then ended up coughing. "Hey, take it easy," Jeff said. "Are you sticking with your Wonder Woman idea?"

"What else? We'll look great together."

Jeff snorted. "I'll bet."

"Thanks a lot," I said. I must have sounded as though I was feeling sorry for myself, because Jeff suddenly said, "Whoa! Have I got the wrong number? I thought I was talking to Vicki Kenyon, all-around whiz kid and Greeley High's woman of the hour."

"Sorry," I said. "I'm afraid you got Wonder Woman instead. She's a bit under the weather these days, but if—" Then I started coughing again, and a chill ran through my body.

Jeff sounded concerned. "Listen," he said, "it sounds like you're pretty sick. I'd better let you get some rest."

"I'm okay," I whispered hoarsely. "At least, I will be by Saturday. I promise you, I won't stand you up."

"Don't worry about Saturday," Jeff said. "If

you're not better by then, Karin can stand in for you at the party."

I could hardly believe my ears. He had to be kidding. If he was, the joke was in very poor taste. "Tell me you were only teasing," I said.

"I wasn't teasing," Jeff said immediately. "I hope you'll get well in time to go to Newport with me. But if you can't, don't worry about it—there'll be other times. The important thing is for you to get well."

I was so outraged that my temperature must have shot up three or four more degrees. "Sure," I said, sarcastically. "And in the meantime, you'll line up good old Karin to take my place."

"Hey," Jeff said, "don't take it personally. Actually, my mother suggested it, but I don't think it's such a bad idea. It would let you off the hook and give Karin a chance to see how beach bums live."

"Oh, fine," I said, fighting back tears. "That's just what I needed to hear. Don't do me any more favors, okay?"

"Wait a minute!" Jeff exclaimed. "What's with you? I'm talking about inviting her just as a friend. Besides, you wanted to get her out of your hair, right?"

By then, tears were streaming down my face. "Are you crazy?" I said loudly. "What I said was that I wanted to spend some time *with* you and *without* her. It sounds to me like you and Karin are trying to get *me* out of *your* hair."

"Hey, take it easy," Jeff said. "I didn't invite Karin in the first place because I knew you'd rather go without her, and I wanted to be alone with you, too. If it turns out that you can't go, I'll really miss you. But I can't help it that you're sick."

"Sure," I retorted. "And I suppose you can't help spending the whole weekend with Karin, either!"

Jeff groaned. I knew I shouldn't have yelled at him, but I was so hurt and furious that I didn't care. How could he even *consider* inviting Karin to take my place? Obviously, he hadn't understood a thing I'd said to him in the past six weeks.

"Look," he said after a minute, "don't you think you're being just a little bit selfish about this?"

"Selfish!" I wailed. "Look who's talking about selfish! You obviously haven't considered *my* feelings at all. Every time I talk to you, all I hear is 'Karin this, Karin that.' Now you're making plans for her to take my place, and I haven't even said I'm not going yet."

"I haven't invited Karin yet, either," Jeff

said evenly. "And if I do, it won't be because I want her to take your place. Why can't you be reasonable about this?"

"Because feelings aren't reasonable," I snapped. "Especially when they're being trampled on. Didn't you want me to tell you when you were being a jerk? Well, I'm telling you now."

After that, Jeff was quiet for a long time. I clutched the phone in one hand and wiped my eyes with the other. I was still shaking, but I wasn't sure whether it was from chills or frustration.

I kept thinking about our last argument, the night we'd run into Karin at McNulty's. We had worked things out that time, and we could do it again, I thought. Any second now, one of us would say, "I'm sorry," and we would make up.

But it won't be me, I added silently. I was the one whose feelings had been hurt, and I just couldn't bring myself to apologize. It would only be a lie. Jeff was the one who was always telling me to admit the truth.

Come on, I thought. *Just say something so we can be friends again.* The silence seemed endless. Just when I thought I couldn't stand it a moment longer, Jeff said, "I like you a lot, Vicki."

"I like you a lot, too," I said, relieved. Everything would be okay now.

Jeff hesitated. "I'm glad," he said finally. "We've had some good times together. But that doesn't mean you own me, and it doesn't mean you can choose my friends."

I was so stunned that I nearly dropped the phone. I'd thought Jeff was about to apologize, and instead he'd practically accused me of trying to run his life. When I finally managed to speak, my voice came out in a squawk. "Yeah, well as long as we're being insulting, I wouldn't want to own you if you were the last boy on earth. And as far as choosing your friends, you can count me out!"

I slammed down the receiver and burst into tears. A few days ago I had never been happier. Even a few minutes ago, being sick had been my biggest problem. Now my life was a total wreck, and I felt so empty that I didn't care whether I was stuck in bed. All I wanted to do was hide under the covers and hope the world would go away.

I buried my face in the pillow and cried until I fell asleep. The next morning, my fight with Jeff seemed like a bad dream. Maybe I had been unfair, I decided. Inviting Karin for Halloween *had* been Jeff's mother's idea, not his. It wasn't his fault that I'd blown up at him when he tried to discuss it.

I knew I had a quick temper, and it had gotten more out of control than usual because I'd had the flu. I was sure that Jeff would understand that. We'd just had a stupid argument because I was sick and he was feeling defensive. The whole thing wasn't important enough to start a world war over. Later, when Jeff got home from school, I would call him and tell him that. Maybe he would even call first.

Once I'd gotten that straight in my mind, life didn't seem quite so hopeless. My temperature was lower, and my mom brought me some orange juice and toast with strawberry preserves. I asked for seconds, then spent the day watching TV, reading, and dozing off.

About four o'clock, Karin peeked her head in the doorway. "You are feeling better?"

"A little," I said. "Come on in."

She sat down in one of my white wicker chairs and started telling me what happened at school. I kept expecting her to tell me that Jeff had invited her to his Halloween party. When she still hadn't mentioned it after half an hour, I wondered if Jeff had changed his mind.

"It looks like I'll be stuck in bed for Halloween," I said. "I guess you'll be going to the dance at school."

Karin's eyes instantly darted away from my face, and my heart sank. "No," she said, looking guilty. "Mrs. Shafer has asked me to spend the weekend with Jeff's family at Newport Beach. It seemed not polite to turn down such a kind invitation."

For a second, I just sat in bed staring at her. I was at a total loss for words. What an idiot I'd been to imagine that Jeff had started seeing things my way! He had arranged to replace me with Karin, after all. And as if that wasn't bad enough, they'd been trying to keep it a secret from me.

I was so furious that I started to shake. "You could have at least told me!" I sputtered, "instead of sneaking around behind my back!"

Karin's mouth fell open in dismay. "But Jeff did tell you, no?"

"All Jeff told me was that he was *thinking* about asking you," I practically yelled. "He was just as afraid to tell me the truth as you were. I bet you two have been secretly planning this all along. You've probably been sneaking around together behind my back ever since I introduced you to each other."

All at once, Karin's eyes flashed angrily. "I think if we are to continue being friends, you had better take care what you say," she said coolly. "I did not come here to be blamed for everything that goes wrong in the life of Vicki Kenyon."

"I'm not blaming you for everything that goes wrong in my life," I snapped. "I'm blaming you for moving in on Jeff."

"You know that is absurd," Karin shot back. "Jeff has become my friend. There is nothing more to it than that."

"Oh, sure! Where have I heard that before?"

Karin jumped to her feet, shaking her head. "Whatever I do, it is all wrong with you. You know I care only for Niels, and still you do not believe that Jeff and I can be friends only."

My face felt hot with fever, and my eyes burned as I glared back at her. "That's what *you* say! You probably made up Niels just like everything else. You had to, because you knew there was no way we could live in the same house after you stole my boyfriend. You even let me think I was crazy to be jealous. And I thought I was getting a sister!"

Karin stared at me for a second, and her face paled. "This whole thing, it is all too crazy," she said. "Why will you not look at the truth?"

She looked as if she was about to cry, but I wasn't going to fall for any more of her tricks. "I've already seen enough," I said, glaring at her. "Just get out of my room and leave me alone!"

Anger showed in Karin's eyes again. "You cannot just—"

"Yes, I can," I yelled, bursting into tears. "I can do anything I want, so *leave me alone!*"

Chapter Ten

Sunday afternoon when Jeff brought Karin home, I was in bed watching television. I heard the front door close, then footsteps came down the hall and someone tapped on my door.

I should have known that Jeff was going to take Karin to Newport Beach whether I liked it or not. But right up until Saturday morning, I'd kept hoping I was wrong. Then I woke up and learned that Jeff and Karin had already left for the beach. What an idiot I had been! It was the most humiliating thing that had ever happened to me.

But by Sunday afternoon, I was through crying about it. No matter what Jeff or Karin said now, it was too late to make up. Even if they knocked on my door all day, I would never have anything to do with either of them again.

I heard still another knock and slid down in the bed, pretending to be asleep. "Vicki? Are you awake?" my mom called.

"Oh, it's you," I said, sitting up against the pillows. "Come on in."

The door opened, and Mom peeked in. "Jeff and Karin are back," she said. "Jeff would like to talk to you."

"Oh, no," I groaned. "I don't want to see him. Tell him to go away."

My mom held the doorknob with one hand and gave me a peculiar look. "This isn't my quarrel," she said after a moment of silence. "Maybe you'd better tell him that yourself."

The next thing I knew she was gone and Jeff had taken her place in the doorway.

"Hi," he said. "How are you feeling?"

I glared at him. "What's it to you?"

He shrugged and smiled, but he seemed more sad than cheerful. "I'm sorry things turned out this way," he said. "So is Karin, but it's really my fault. It's true that my mom invited her to the party, but when you got so huffy about it . . ." He paused and shrugged his shoulders again. "Well, I'm kind of touchy

114

about being told whom to spend my time with. But you already know how stubborn I can be. I guess I just let things get out of hand this time."

"Yeah," I shot back, "I guess you did." I tried to sound cutting, but I could barely look at Jeff without crying. I kept imagining him and Karin together at the Halloween party, and that reminded me of the night I'd danced with him at his back-to-school party. I could almost feel the easy way we had moved together and the warmth of Jeff's arm against my waist. But from now on Karin would be in his arms, and not me.

I felt so depressed and humiliated at the thought that I couldn't stand to be in the same room with him. "Look," I said, "this is going nowhere. Why don't you just leave?"

Jeff hesitated and then sat down in one of my wicker chairs. "I know you're mad at me," he said. "But you're mad for the wrong reason. There is nothing between me and Karin. I hardly saw her all weekend. She spent most of her time with my cousin Lisa."

"Sure," I said sarcastically. "And I suppose there *is* something between you and me."

Jeff's eyes flashed with anger. "There *was*," he said coldly. "But that was before I found out what you're really like."

"Oh, yeah? And what *am* I really like?"

Jeff looked at me for a long time, as though he were seriously considering my question. Then a lopsided smile came over his face. "Listen," he said, "we're both saying things we don't mean. If we're not careful, it'll be too late to take them back."

"It was already too late when you and Karin left for Newport Beach," I said miserably.

"I told you that didn't mean anything," Jeff protested.

"Oh, right." Tears flooded down my cheeks. "It didn't mean anything to *you*, maybe. What it meant to me was that you care more about Karin's feelings than mine."

"I don't get it," Jeff said, throwing up his hands. "I've been trying to take everyone's feelings into account, but you seem to think your feelings are more important than anyone else's."

That was the most outrageous thing he'd said yet. I'd spent the past two months thinking about other people's feelings. I had worried about Karin fitting in, about Nancy resenting her being around, about Don passing his exam, and about Jeff thinking I was selfish. Now, all I wanted was for someone to think about *my* feelings for a change.

Suddenly, my head was pounding and a

hot flush spread up my neck. "How would you know what I think?"

Jeff clenched and unclenched one hand in frustration. "Lately the only thing you seem to be feeling is jealousy," he said. "Maybe that's not something I want to encourage. One of the things that attracted me to you in the first place was your independence."

"Oh, great!" I snapped. "First you order me to say what I really mean instead of what I think you want to hear. Then as soon as I do, you decide you don't like it. So why don't you just get out of my bedroom and go talk to Karin? Maybe she'll tell you something you want to hear!"

Jeff stared back at me, obviously confused. "Maybe you've got a point," he said cautiously. "But just because you admit you're jealous, it doesn't mean I have to like—"

"Oh!" His condescending tone made me so furious that I couldn't stand to listen to him for another second. "I don't care if you like *any*thing about me," I shouted. "And I don't want to talk about it anymore. This discussion is *over*. Just get out of here and out of my life."

Jeff looked startled and a little hurt. "Okay," he said, slowly getting to his feet. "If that's how you really feel, I guess there's nothing I can do about it. But you're not being fair to Karin. She needs you to help her, not resent her. She's really upset that you're giving her the cold shoulder. I feel as if it's all my fault . . ."

When I heard that, I went off like Mount Vesuvius. "I'm tired of hearing about Karin!" I screamed. "Particularly from you. Now if you don't mind . . ."

I slid back down in the bed and rolled over to face the wall. The room was so quiet that I could hear the sheets rustle. Then Jeff sighed and retreated across my white carpet. The door closed softly behind him, and my room suddenly seemed very empty. I pressed my face into the pillow, where the crazy beat of my heart echoed in my ears. It was pounding so hard that I was sure it would either explode with anger or break in misery.

Chapter Eleven

Some people say the seasons don't change much in Southern California. Maybe they're right, but by mid-November, the summer was definitely gone. Even on sunny days, kids were wearing light sweaters, and the air had that cool, crisp feel that makes me think of pumpkin pie and stuffed turkey.

Nancy must have been feeling the autumn air, too. "What are you going to do over the Thanksgiving holiday?" she asked as we walked out of our one-thirty chemistry class.

"Just hang around at home, I guess. Every year, we cook a huge dinner and invite a couple of my parents' friends." I pushed up the sleeves of my blue angora sweater and wrinkled my nose. "Usually it's a lot of fun, but I'm not really looking forward to it this year."

Nancy frowned. "Because of Karin?"

"Yeah," I said. "I can't exactly imagine kidding around in the kitchen, baking pies and stuff, with her there."

"It probably won't be much fun for her, either," Nancy pointed out. "Did you ever think of that?"

"*She's* the one who should have thought of it," I retorted, "before she decided to get cozy with Jeff."

Nancy looked at me with disapproving eyes. I automatically started feeling defensive, the way I always did when I sensed that she was about to start lecturing me. But she just jerked her head toward the drinking fountain and said, "Speaking of which . . ."

I looked up the hall and saw Jeff staring back at me. During the week and a half since Halloween, I had been carefully avoiding him. Now, the sight of his brown eyes and dark spiky hair brought a flash of warmth to my cheeks. "Speaking of *whom*," I told Nancy, trying to seem casual. "Come on, let's go in the rest room."

We ducked through the door and walked

over to the mirror. Three girls were already there, applying lipstick and mascara. I took out my brush and started fluffing the front of my hair.

"Have you ever considered that you might be wrong about him?" Nancy asked, rummaging through her nylon bag. "I mean, Jeff is usually such a straightforward guy. Why would he have lied to you about Karin?"

I sighed. Maybe the real problem was that I'd started thinking of Jeff as my boyfriend. That meant I treated him in a special way and expected him to do the same. He hadn't tried to discourage me. In fact, he'd led me on—until Karin entered the picture, that is. Even if Jeff was telling the truth that he and Karin weren't involved, they were still more loyal to each other than they were to me. That was what really hurt, I decided, as I finished arranging my bangs.

But how could I explain that to Nancy? Just like Jeff and my mom, she'd say I was being jealous and unreasonable.

I pulled my hair back over my shoulders and glanced at Nancy in the mirror. For a second, I thought she might have forgotten what she'd asked me. Judging by the relaxed and unconcerned expression on her face, I assumed the discussion was over and I'd been let off easy. I should have known better.

"You still haven't answered," Nancy said as she leaned closer to the mirror. "Why would Jeff say that about Karin if he didn't mean it?"

I turned to my friend and sighed. "Maybe he did tell me the truth," I said. "But anyone can see he's more concerned about Karin than me. He might have lied to protect her, because he was afraid I'd blame her for moving in on him."

Nancy continued to apply her orchid lipstick without blinking an eye. "I can't believe someone as smart as you could come up with such a dumb explanation, Vicki," she said. "But even if Jeff lied for that reason, well, in a way, he'd be right. I mean, you've barely spoken to Karin since she got back from Newport." She gave me a long look, then reached for a paper towel to blot her lipstick.

"Well I can't help it," I said, wishing I didn't sound so defensive. "How would *you* feel if you had to live with a traitor?"

"You don't know she's a traitor," Nancy said, dropping her lipstick back in her bag. "Everyone but you believes that she and Jeff are just friends."

"Yeah, I know," I said. "So why can't I just be sensible about it, the way *you* would be, huh?"

Nancy shrugged. "Maybe I would be. You're just driving yourself crazy. Why can't you admit you made a mistake?"

I rolled my eyes at her. That was exactly what I had expected Nancy to say. No matter how many times I explained it, no one seemed to understand my situation. "Look," I said patiently, "maybe I was wrong to think Jeff and Karin had a case on each other. But that doesn't matter. What bothers me is that Jeff seems more loyal to her than he is to me. I mean, what's the point of being someone's girlfriend if he puts everyone else ahead of you?"

Nancy paused. "I guess I see what you mean," she said after a minute. "But maybe that's just how Jeff is. Why take it out on Karin?"

"Oh, come on!" I blurted out. "Karin was supposed to be my friend. She didn't have to let things get out of hand. How would you feel if I treated Gary the way Karin treats Jeff?"

Nancy's eyes lit up as though she were ready to pounce. "I've already told you the answer to that," she said. "As long as we weren't going steady, it wouldn't be any of my business. Gary has the right to see anyone he wants, and so does Jeff."

"Yeah," I said, "but how would you *feel* about it? Don't tell me it wouldn't bother you if Gary and I started hanging out together."

"It might get to me," Nancy said. "It would probably even hurt. But that doesn't mean I would stop being friends with you. If you deliberately tried to steal him, that would be rotten. But if he just liked being with you, it wouldn't be anyone's fault."

"Thanks," I said sarcastically. "It's so comforting to hear that. Fortunately for you, I'm not as irresistible as Karin. She's so gorgeous and popular that she doesn't need me, anyway."

At that point, Nancy stared at me hard, as if she'd just had a revelation. "I never really thought about that," she said. "You really envy Karin, don't you? I bet you'd be jealous of her even if you'd never met Jeff."

There it was again—no matter how I explained the situation, everyone always decided it was somehow my fault. I sighed, thinking I'd had enough of Nancy's theories for one day. "That's really deep," I said. "Now let's get going, or I'll be late for class again."

* * *

For almost the entire hour of our history class that afternoon, I could feel Karin's eyes on me. Sensing that she was up to something, I deliberately avoided her gaze, and when the bell rang, I quickly gathered up my books and hurried out of the room. But I didn't move fast enough. By the time I'd reached the hallway, Karin was at my side.

"Are you going home now?" she asked. "I thought we might walk together."

I started to say "forget it," but for some reason, I didn't. Karin was wearing a new pink sweater and wool skirt that should have made her look terrific, yet her skin seemed unusually pale, and her huge blue eyes were red and tired-looking. In fact, she seemed so depressed that I couldn't help thinking about my talk with Nancy.

"Thanksgiving probably won't be much fun for Karin, either," Nancy had said. *"Did you ever think of that?"* To be perfectly honest, I *had* thought about it, and I'd actually hoped that Karin would spend Thanksgiving and every other day of the year feeling as miserable as I did.

Judging by the way Karin looked that day, my wish had come true. Somehow, that didn't make me as happy as I'd imagined it would. Instead, I felt sorry for her and a little ashamed of myself. I still didn't think I'd really been unfair to her, but maybe she had suffered enough. Even though I have a quick temper, I've never been able to carry a grudge for very long. Besides, I realized now, my real feud was with Jeff. He was the one who had insisted on including Karin in all our activities.

All Karin had done was try to fit in and make friends. Oh, sure, she could have had the tact to say no now and then. But wanting to have a good time was hardly a crime. And even if she had gotten in the way of my love life, I wasn't in the habit of letting my whole life revolve around boys. And Jeff Shafer wasn't the only fish in the sea.

Maybe Nancy was right, I decided. It was about time to forgive Karin and get on with my life. Walking home together would be a good start, but I had to stay at school for an extra tutoring session with Don Bradley. I was trying to think of a friendly way to tell Karin that when Jeff walked up. The instant Karin saw him, a look of relief came over her face. Jeff smiled back at her, and there was something strange about his expression, too. Watching them gave me a fresh attack of jealousy, but I ignored it and said, "Hi."

"Hi," Jeff replied easily. "Basketball practice is off for today. Can I give you two a ride home?"

Karin nodded and gave me a questioning look. *Oh great,* I thought instantly. Just like old times. Only now, I was the one who made it three's-a-crowd.

A minute earlier I had felt sorry for Karin, and I had stupidly imagined that she needed me. Now it was very obvious that she preferred being with Jeff. She only wanted to walk home with me because she had thought he had basketball practice. And it was just as obvious that Jeff had come looking for Karin, not me. "Thanks," I replied coolly. "But I've already got plans."

I turned and headed for the ESL classroom before Jeff or Karin could say another word. When I arrived, Don was already there, slouched in a chair with his feet propped up on the table where we worked.

"Hi," I said, setting down my books and hoping I didn't sound as depressed as I felt.

Don swung his feet off the table and grinned cheerfully. "Man, am I glad to see you! I was afraid you'd forgotten me."

"Sorry I'm late," I said. "I got held up." I dropped into the chair next to Don. He always had a way of making me feel needed and cared about. After my run-in with Jeff and Karin, the sight of his big frame and warm smile was definitely comforting. I could tell from his voice that he really was glad to see me, too.

I smiled back at Don, thinking how nice it was to feel important to someone. Suddenly I felt tears springing to my eyes. It was embarrassing the way I was always crying lately. I picked up a spiral notebook and ducked behind it to hide my face, but it was too late. Don had already seen me starting to cry.

"Hey," he said, gently pulling the notebook out of my hands. "What's the matter, Vicki?"

I shrugged and dabbed at my eyes, trying to get myself under control. Then Don pulled a huge white handkerchief out of the pocket of his jeans and held it out to me. The sight of Don Bradley—the toughest football player Greeley High had ever known—with a sparkling white hankie in his hand and a tender, sympathetic look in his ice-blue eyes nearly made me laugh in spite of my misery.

Don gave a tight little smile, as if he knew the joke was on him. "Okay. All right. Go on and laugh. I just thought maybe you'd want to wipe your eyes. If you want to laugh at me instead, that's just as good."

"Just as well," I said, taking his handkerchief. I was so used to correcting him that my words came out automatically. Somehow that was even funnier than the handkerchief. We both laughed, and my eyes filled with tears again. I ducked my head in embarrassment, but Don just bent down and looked up into my face.

"Hey, come on," he said softly. "You and Jeff on the outs again, or what?"

He was being so sweet that I wanted to hug him. For a second, I wondered if I could be in love with him instead of Jeff. It definitely would have been easier. Don was so open and easy to understand; and he seemed to be the only person in the world who understood me. But as much as I like Don, I never felt that special thrill with him that I felt with Jeff.

Not that it made any difference now. I sighed loudly and wiped my eyes with Don's handkerchief. "Yeah," I said. "Things aren't working out too well between us."

Don looked baffled. "Man, you two seem perfect together. If you ask me, Jeff ought to have his head examined."

I gave a wry smile. "It's nice to know there's at least one person on my side. Everyone else think's *I'm* the one who's out of line."

"Yeah, well the game can get rough sometimes. But you don't have to let it get you down." He patted my shoulder, looking a little embarrassed. "Hey, listen. Why not come out to Newport Beach with me this Saturday? If the weather's lousy, we can hang out at the arcade or take in a movie."

I hesitated, not sure how to take the invitation. It wouldn't be fair to go out on a date with Don, considering that I didn't like him in a romantic way. On the other hand, I was feeling pretty lonely lately, and Don was definitely good company.

"I don't know," I said after a minute. "I mean, I'm not really sure about anything right now."

Don shrugged and looked down at his feet. "Hey, just thought it might cheer you up," he said. "That's what buddies are for. Besides, after everything you've done for me, it's the least I can do in return."

That was the nicest thing anyone had said to me in a long time. "You've cheered me up already," I said, smiling warmly. "Maybe you're right. I should be out having fun instead of letting things get me down so much."

"For an English tutor, you sure don't speak very clearly," Don teased. "Did that mean yes or no?"

130

"Sorry," I said. "It definitely means yes."

"Great," Don said. "I'll pick you up around ten on Saturday morning. Now let's get to work. If I flunk my next English exam, I'm going to be the one who needs cheering up."

Chapter Twelve

Saturday morning while I was getting ready to go to the beach with Don, Karin came and stood in the bathroom doorway. During the first couple of weeks she had lived with me, she had done that often. In fact, we both had. Whenever one of us was dressing or fixing her hair, the other would stand around talking, giving advice, or helping.

Now, seeing her standing in the doorway reminded me again of how much I had enjoyed being with her. For a moment I wished we could be friends again. But I had felt the same way last Wednesday, and all it had gotten me was another slap in the face. Now I was determined not to fall into the same trap again. "Do you need the bathroom?" I asked, barely glancing away from the mirror.

Karin shook her head, then started to say something and stopped. I gave her a suspicious look and turned on the hair dryer. I figured she would leave when she realized I was ignoring her. Instead she leaned against the door frame, folded her arms across her chest, and sighed. "You have a date with Don Bradley?" she asked loudly over the hum of the hair dryer.

It's none of your business, I wanted to say. But no matter how much I resented Karin, I couldn't be quite *that* rude, so I shrugged casually and turned off the hair dryer. "Sort of," I said. "We're just going out to Newport Beach."

Karin looked back at me as if her worst suspicions had come true. "But you should be with Jeff," she said. "Now you are ending up with Don, and I am to blame. It is all my fault."

"It doesn't have anything to do with you," I said. "It just so happens that Don is a sweet guy, and we have some good times together."

I must not have sounded very convincing, because Karin looked doubtful. "For sure, Don is a nice boy," she said. "But I think he is not one to take the place of Jeff Shafer."

I gave an exasperated sigh. "Nobody's taking anybody's place," I said. "I just feel like getting out and having some fun for a change. What difference does it make, anyway? Jeff and I are through. *You* ought to know that better than anybody."

Karin shook her head vehemently. "You are right that I ought to know better than anybody, but you are wrong about Jeff. He is my friend and tells me much of what is in his heart. What he tells me is *not* that he wishes that you and he would be through. Why can you not believe me when I tell you this?"

"Why should I believe you? You and Jeff are so thick, you would say anything. Why don't you just quit faking it and admit how you really feel about each other?" I blurted the words out without thinking, and I didn't care. If what Karin had said was true, why didn't Jeff tell *me* what was "in his heart" instead of telling her?

Karin just stood there shaking her head, as if she were talking to herself. "She is so smart, this Vicki Kenyon, when it is about her schoolwork. But when it comes to Jeff Shafer, she is—what do you say? A complete dodo."

I wasn't sure whether to scream or giggle. For a second, I stared at her with my mouth hanging open in astonishment. "And just what is that supposed to mean?" I demanded.

" 'What is that supposed to mean?' " Karin repeated, imitating my tone of voice and looking frustrated. "For you, everything must be an explanation. You are like my boyfriend—always demanding an explanation and asking why. 'Why should I believe? What difference does it make? What does it mean?' Yet you believe nothing you are told."

She made it sound so tragic that my temper subsided. "Look," I said, "I miss having you for a friend, and I miss seeing Jeff. I wish I *could* believe you, and it's not as if I haven't tried. But when I see the way you two look at each other, it's pretty hard to believe there's nothing between you."

Karin shook her head again, gazing past me, then she looked me straight in the eye and smiled sadly. "I don't ask you to believe there is nothing between us," she said. "But as I have told you before, it is only friendship. Jeff has been kind to me at times when I have been very lonely. I have tried to be his friend in return, and be your friend, too. That has not been so easy."

I stared at her in confusion. In some ways, I knew she really had tried to be my friend, and I hadn't always made it easy for her. But what did she expect? I had imagined she would be like a sister—someone to talk to and share good times with, and most of all, someone to rely on.

Instead, she had become the center of attention, leaving me out in the cold. My friends were crazy about her, my parents always took her side, and she looked better in my clothes than I did. I could have coped with all that, but I drew the line at her taking over Jeff. Whether she only thought of him as a friend or not, she shouldn't have crowded in on him.

"Yeah, well, I'm sorry about the way things have turned out," I said at last. "But it hasn't been so easy for me, either. You and Jeff have each other now, so what do you need me for, anyway?"

"You cannot be serious!" Karin exclaimed, her eyes opening wide with horror. "I do not take your place with Jeff, nor does he take your place with me. We both miss you very much." All at once, her shoulders slumped and a discouraged look came over her face. "But what is the point of telling you all this yet another time?" she said sadly. "You are as stubborn as Jeff."

She turned and walked away without another word. I stared after her in astonishment, then I started worrying. It wasn't like Karin to be so curt and reckless. No matter how hurt or upset *I* had felt in the last few weeks, she had generally seemed carefree and cheerful.

The doorbell rang, and I drew my comb through my hair one last time. If my life had become this complicated in only sixteen years, what would it be like when I was twenty-five? I wondered as I went to the door.

"Hi," Don said, smiling cheerfully. "Ready to hit the road?"

After all my confusion around Jeff and Karin, Don's big, expressive face with its wide smile and frank blue eyes was a welcome sight. "Yeah," I said, feeling instantly relaxed. "Just let me grab a sweater."

A few minutes later we were riding down the freeway in Don's beat-up Datsun pickup. "This is really nice of you," I said. "I was afraid I was forgetting how to have fun."

"Hey," Don said, "that's what friends are for. You know, helping keep your head on straight, and all that."

I grinned, thinking he really was one of the nicest guys I had ever known. We started talking about football and some of the kids we both knew, then before I knew it, we were parking near the boardwalk at Newport. The sun was high overhead by then, but the day was too foggy to be really warm. I pulled on my sweater as we climbed out of the truck, then we stood watching the sailboats and windsurfers near the docks.

"Man," Don said, "that windsurfing is my kind of sport. Have you ever tried it?"

I shook my head, watching a boy balance on his surfboard and swing the sail to catch the breeze. "Huh-uh," I said. "It looks too hard for me."

"It's not so hard once you get the hang of it," Don said. "I'll teach you if you want." Then he smiled, looking oddly pleased with himself. "Hey, that would be a switch! I never thought I'd be offering to tutor you."

Just then, a gust of wind caught the sail of the surfboard. The board tilted suddenly, dumping its rider into the chilly water. "No thanks!" I said, laughing. "I know you'd be a great tutor, but I like my sports a little warmer."

Don laughed and pulled on his jacket. "Man,

maybe you've got a point. That's enough fresh air for one day. Let's head over to the arcade and get out of this wind."

At the arcade, we ran into some friends of Don's and challenged them to a video game tournament. Around one o'clock the other kids left, and Don and I went to get a pizza. "Hey, this is great, isn't it?" Don said, as we sat down in a wooden booth. "We ought to come out here more often."

I hesitated. The day had been going great, except that almost everything we did in Newport Beach reminded me of Jeff. This was where I had first introduced him to Karin. It was also where Karin had spent Halloween with him while I was sick in bed. I'd even been daydreaming that I was there with Jeff instead of Don.

"Yeah," I said at last. "If only it didn't bring back so many bad memories."

Don looked sympathetic. "You and Jeff, you mean?" I shrugged and nodded, not wanting to bore him with my problems. "Hey, man, it's okay," he said. "You can't expect to forget him overnight."

I sighed and leaned my chin on my hand. "I guess so, but I'm not sure anymore whether I want to forget him or he wants to forget me.

I've been convinced he has a case on Karin, but everyone says I'm crazy. Lately, I'm beginning to wonder if they're right."

"Whoa," Don said. He took a long sip of his Coke, then sat back in his seat. "I *know* you're not crazy, but it seems to me you've been talking to everyone but the right person. What does Jeff have to say about all this?"

At that, my face turned red with embarrassment. "That's just the trouble," I admitted. "He says Karin is just a friend, but how he acts is something else. I mean, he pays more attention to her than me, but if I try to talk about it, we always end up fighting. Everything he says just makes me more jealous of Karin. Then he gets mad at me for being jealous and starts defending her." I shrugged with frustration. "The crazy thing is, I was never the jealous type until Karin came here. Now sometimes I get so resentful and competitive that I hardly recognize myself."

A waiter arrived with our pizza. I put a slice on my plate to cool, while Don picked up a huge slab and nibbled at the edges. He had a serious expression on his face, as if pondering an important matter. "I guess I know what you mean about hardly recognizing yourself," he said after a minute. "In a way, the same thing happened to me when I first made the football squad. Before that, I was always big on team play. Then all of a sudden, I was so hot to prove myself that I couldn't stand to see anyone else carry the ball."

He shook his head and grinned sheepishly. "There I was, this dumb rookie, competing with my own teammates. Man, that got me nowhere fast. Pretty soon, I started thinking my own men were out to get me. I still get embarrassed just thinking about it."

He took a long swallow from his Coke and a huge bite of pizza. I watched him, wondering how his story related to me and Karin. "I don't get it," I finally said. "You think I'm jealous of Karin because I want to have all the attention?"

Don's cheeks turned beet red. "Hey, Vicki, man—is that how I came across? I guess what I really meant was, sometimes the competition is all in your own mind. I mean, I didn't have to prove anything to those guys. They accepted me the minute I made the team—until I started putting the press on them, anyway. After that, they came down on me hard and fast."

"What happened then?" I asked.

Don grinned back at me as he reached for

another slice of pizza. "I got real humble. And you know what? I ended up being Greeley's star quarterback. As long as I fought my own men, they had to fight me back. But as soon as they saw me playing for the team instead of myself, they backed me all the way."

"You know," I began, taking a bite of my pizza, "Jeff said something like that about basketball, too. Well, not exactly, but he said it only looks as if he's the star of the team. The other guys really do all the work."

"Yeah," Don said. "You make the other guys look good, they'll do the same for you. Make them look bad . . ." He drew one finger across the front of his neck, like a knife cutting his throat. "Something to think about, anyway. Listen, I've got a date tonight, so we'd better take off soon."

A date? I thought in surprise. Even though I only liked Don as a friend, it had somehow made me feel good to think that he liked me as more. *Well, my first lesson in how to be humble,* I thought wryly. "Sure, I'm ready when you are," I said. "Are you going to tell me who you're going out with, or is it a big secret?"

All at once, his blue eyes lit up like ocean water in the morning sunlight. "Kaye Raymond," he said. "Maybe you know her. She just transferred from across town, but she's on the varsity pep squad."

Although I hadn't met Kaye yet, I had seen her around school. She was about my size, but more athletic. She came across as independent, yet also gentle and cuddly. *Just the kind of girl I would have picked for Don*, I thought. "Yeah," I told him, nodding enthusiastically. "She's really cute. I haven't actually met her yet, but from what I've seen of her, she seems nice."

Don's smile suddenly turned shy. "Yeah, she is nice," he said. "I'm glad you think so, too."

"Who knows?" I said, winking at him and sliding out of the booth. "Maybe we'll end up double-dating some time, huh?"

Don unfolded himself from his seat, looking thoughtful. I knew what he was thinking, because I was thinking it, too. Neither of us was used to being close friends with someone of the opposite sex. The idea of double-dating together seemed odd, yet it somehow seemed natural, too. At least, it did to me.

Don looked as if he wasn't so sure. Finally he gave another one of his shy grins. "Yeah, sure. Maybe we will. If you and Jeff ever get your act together."

I decided to let that pass, but all the way home I kept thinking about what Don had said about competing with his own teammates. In a way, what had happened to him was a lot like what had happened with me and Karin. At first, I had seen the two of us as a team, then she instantly became popular, and I started feeling left out. After that, I thought of her more as a rival than a friend.

But maybe the competition was all in my own mind. I had always felt secure and confident because I was an only child and had always been the focus of attention. Then along came Karin, and I suddenly felt so insecure and jealous that I had imagined she was deliberately upstaging me. Was it possible I had only imagined her moving in on Jeff, too?

I glanced over at Don, feeling like a total idiot. We had just spent the whole day together, yet we were just good friends. If Don and I could be buddies, why couldn't Jeff and Karin be, too?

By the time Don pulled up in front of my house, I had made up my mind to try to make up with Jeff and Karin. At the thought of a reconciliation, I felt happier than I had felt since the day Don passed his English exam.

"Thanks," I told him as I stepped out of his

truck, "for cheering me up and helping me get my head on straight."

"Hey, man, it's nothing," Don said with a shrug. "See you later."

"Yeah. Have a nice time with Kaye. I have a feeling we might be thinking about double-dating sometime soon."

Don grinned, but before he had time to say anything, I turned and ran up the sidewalk to my house. If Karin was home, I could talk to her right away. Maybe I could even call Jeff this evening, too.

I burst through the front door, then I heard voices coming from the living room and hesitated.

"I don't know what to do," Karin was saying. "Love seems only to make trouble. The whole year I so much looked forward to, now it has all gone wrong."

She sounded so miserable that my heart went out to her. This should have been one of the happiest times in her life, but I had turned it into a nightmare for her. Suddenly, I was more determined than ever to apologize and make things right. I rushed into the living room, then froze with shock.

Jeff and Karin were sitting together on the couch, facing away from me. Jeff's arm was around Karin, and she was leaning her head on his shoulder.

I stared at them in disbelief, feeling more and more outraged by the second. My knees went weak, and the back of my neck felt as if it were on fire. Finally I let out a loud gasp. The noise must have startled Jeff and Karin. They both jumped and looked around at me at the same instant.

For a second I just stood there shaking my head and feeling as if I had just walked into a nightmare. Tears streamed down my face. "I don't believe this," I whispered. "Just when I decided I was wrong. . . ."

My voice choked up, and I broke off. I had spent the whole afternoon blaming myself for not trusting them. Suddenly I couldn't stand to look at them a moment longer. I dashed to my room, locked the door behind me, and flung myself down on my bed.

Almost immediately, I heard someone running down the hall after me. Then Karin was calling my name and knocking on my door. "Vicki, please. Open the door. It is not what you think."

"Oh, sure," I screamed at her through the door. "I'm sick of your lies, Karin. Do you know I was actually feeling sorry for you a minute ago. I even blamed myself. Well, you two have made a fool of me for the last time."

After that, Karin was silent for a while. Just when I thought maybe she had gone away, she said, "I do not blame you, Vicki. I know how it must look, but please—give me a chance to explain to you."

"Forget it!" I shot back. "I wanted a sister, and all I got was a traitor. That's all the explanation I need. Just go away and leave me alone!"

Chapter Thirteen

I stayed in my room the rest of the night. After a while my mom came to call me to dinner, and when I told her I wasn't hungry, she tried to persuade me to let her come in. Normally, she was the best person to talk to when I was upset, but right then I couldn't even face her.

All I could think about was seeing Jeff and Karin together. I had spent the whole afternoon blaming myself for not trusting them. I had swallowed my pride and decided to apologize. Then I had walked in and found them in each other's arms!

I was so upset that I put on my pajamas and went to sleep. When I woke up the next morning, I was still miserable. In addition, I was starving, but I knew everyone would be sitting around in the kitchen reading the Sunday newspaper and having a late breakfast. I couldn't bear the thought of even seeing Karin, so I stayed in bed, flipping through the channels on my TV to keep my mind off my stomach and everything else.

That might have worked, except that I hadn't eaten anything since Don and I had had lunch at Newport Beach the day before. After seeing three hamburger commercials and two ice-cream ads, I decided that I couldn't stand it any longer. I considered calling from my phone to ask my mom to bring me some breakfast, but I knew she'd never let me get away with that. Besides, what if Karin happened to answer the phone?

I groaned and rolled out of bed. Unless I planned to starve to death, I couldn't stay in my room forever. Maybe Karin had left the kitchen by now, I thought hopefully. With any luck, she might even have left the house.

I put on my robe and walked quietly down the hall. As I passed the living room, I glanced through the door and saw Karin sitting on the couch reading a book. With a sigh of relief, I went on to the kitchen, fixed a ham and cheese sandwich, and sat down to eat.

The next thing I knew, Karin was there at the table, pulling out a chair to sit down across from me. Only a moment before I'd been starving. Now my stomach was churning so violently that I wasn't sure I could choke down any food at all. I ignored Karin and forced myself to bite into my sandwich.

"You will not even look at me," I heard Karin say. "Can it be so bad as all that?"

I went on chewing as if she weren't there, but ignoring her wasn't easy. Although I had a quick temper, I wasn't in the habit of being deliberately rude. Now I figured I didn't have any choice. Karin was determined to talk to me, and anything she said would only make things worse.

"You don't understand," she exclaimed angrily. "It is Niels, not Jeff."

She sounded exactly the way I felt—angry and hurt. I looked up at her in astonishment. Karin was staring down at the table with her arms crossed tightly across her chest. "He has just written me that he has found another girl," she said so softly that I could barely hear her.

For a split second, I was almost happy. *It served her right,* I thought, after the torment she'd put me through over Jeff. But I was immediately ashamed of myself. Karen looked so totally wretched that even I couldn't help feeling sorry for her. Tears were streaming down her face, and her words came out in a painful rush.

"It is what I feared would happen," she sobbed. "But what can I do? I am so far away, without even my family or friends to turn to. My whole life is nothing but strangeness. Even the language I speak is not my own. Now I have not even you for my friend, and I have gotten only more trouble for talking with Jeff."

She paused, rubbing her eyes with her fists. "Go to America," she went on bitterly, "that is what they told me, my friends back at home. It is the opportunity of a lifetime, they said, and to be an exchange student is a great honor. Pagh! America is beautiful, but for me to come here was a terrible mistake. I wish nothing so much as to be back home, with my own family who loves me and my friends who understand."

Tears streamed down Karin's cheeks again. She threw her arms down on the table and buried her face in them.

I stared at her in dismay, so stunned that I couldn't move. I kept seeing an image of her the day we picked her up at the airport. With her stylish miniskirt and chic hairstyle, she had looked incredibly sophisticated and confident. From the very first moment, she had joked and flirted like every other girl I knew. All my friends liked her, and she had been an instant success at Greeley High. Everything she touched seemed to turn to gold.

I had been so envious of Karin that it had never really occurred to me that she might be as insecure as I was. Now I began to understand that the past couple of months had been hard on her, too. She looked poised and glamorous, but she was still just a sixteen-year-old girl like me. She had all the same doubts and problems I had, plus she was thousands of miles from home. Karin had no one to rely on but me.

No wonder Karin had been seeing so much of Jeff! He'd been there for her when she couldn't talk to *me* about anything. I should have realized that all along, but I was so blind with jealousy that I couldn't think straight. Now Niels had broken up with her, and Jeff had had to comfort her.

I was so ashamed that tears came to my own eyes. Karin was still sitting with her head on her arms, sobbing miserably. My heart went out to her, and I walked around the table and put my arms around her shoulders. "I didn't know," I said. "I'm very sorry about Niels."

For a second Karin only cried harder. I could feel her shoulders shaking, and I started to draw away, thinking I was only making her feel worse. Then she wiped her face back and forth on her arms and lifted her head. She seemed a little calmer, but her eyes were red and swollen, and her cheeks were damp and flushed. I grabbed a handful of paper towels from over the kitchen sink and pressed them into her hands.

"I really am sorry about Niels," I said again. "And everything else, too. I've been acting like a real jerk."

Karin wiped her face with the towels, then blew her nose loudly. Tears filled her eyes again, but she managed to smile weakly. "I am the one to apologize," she said softly. "To make such trouble in the home where I am a guest. I am a very poor ambassador for my country. You will think the Norwegians an ungrateful people, no? I meant not to offend, but only—"

"Shh," I said, putting my hand back on her shoulder. "It's not your fault. It's just that I never considered all the ways I would be sharing my life with you. Even though I knew it was selfish, I couldn't help resenting you sometimes. Then when you and Jeff started getting along so well, it was the last straw. I wanted him to myself, and it seemed as if you were always there."

Karin's eyes widened in amazement. "But if only I had known!" she exclaimed. "I thought it was what Americans do—all going around, boys and girls together. I, too, need at times to be alone, but I feared to—bow out? Wanting not to be impolite in not accepting the arrangements of my host."

At that point, it was my turn to look astonished. "You mean you thought you had to go along with me all the time? Because you thought I expected it?"

Karin nodded, looking embarrassed. "Yes, and I am ashamed, knowing now what you think. And, too, I wanted to see as much as possible of American life—to tell of it when I returned home. It is like a job, being an exchange student. You are expected to do so much."

"Oh, no," I said, walking around the table and dropping back into my chair. "The whole time I was going out of my mind resenting you, and you were trying to be a good guest. I feel like a complete idiot."

"Perhaps you were a little bit the idiot," Karin said. "But the complete idiot was me. After a time, I saw that you were disturbed by my friendship with Jeff. But he was so kind to me that I did not wish to turn away from him."

"He probably wouldn't have let you, anyway," I said, recalling all the arguments Jeff and I had had over Karin. "He knew how jealous I was, and he was determined not to give in to me. As if he thought I actually *liked* the way I was behaving!" I added, blushing with embarrassment.

Karin looked sympathetic. "You must not be so hard on yourself," she said. "It is all a misunderstanding."

I nodded. "Karin, I know I've given you a really hard time, but I hope you'll stay and give us a chance to work things out." I smiled ruefully. "I always wanted a sister, and I still do. Only now, I think, I know a little more about what having one means."

Karin gave a short laugh, but her face looked serious. "If only you are certain you wish to have me, I will be happy to stay. At home, too, it would be very difficult now. Always, I should imagine coming across Niels with his new girl. . . ."

She broke off, and tears glistened in the corners of her eyes.

"Do you think there's any chance he might change his mind?" I asked. "Maybe he just got lonely because you're so far away."

"I have thought that myself," Karin said. "But loneliness did not make me turn away from him in only a few weeks. I am sad to lose him, yet it is well to know now that his heart wanders so quickly, no?"

"I guess you're right," I said, sighing and thinking of Jeff again. "Sometimes a relationship seems totally perfect, and then you discover something between you that makes it all wrong. Maybe if that has to happen, though, the sooner you find out, the better off you are."

"Exactly," said Karin. "But even then, it is painful to accept. As with you and Jeff, no? Do you think now you will call him and make things okay?"

I shook my head. I was less certain than ever about my relationship with Jeff. In many ways, I still thought he was the most perfect boy I could ever hope to meet, but I also knew that we had some very different ideas about what we should expect from each other.

"I don't know," I replied at last. "In a way, Jeff and I are like you and Niels. No matter how much we care about each other, there are some things that just don't work." *And,* I added silently, *I still don't have any idea how he feels about me.*

Chapter Fourteen

"I thought for sure I would have seen Jeff by now," I said as Karin and Nancy and I walked out of the cafeteria Monday. "Maybe he didn't come to school today."

"I know he's here," said Nancy. "I saw him at his locker on my way to English class. Maybe he went off-campus for lunch."

"Or else he's trying to avoid me," I said. Before leaving for school that morning, I had made up my mind to talk to Jeff. I knew it was going to be hard, even if he was willing to cooperate. But having him avoid me was the last thing I needed. Just thinking about it made my stomach queasy.

Karin seemed to be reading my mind. "I do

not think he is avoiding you," she said. "If he is, I am sure it would be for a reason other than what you might think."

"Such as?" Nancy asked, giving Karin a curious look. We stopped as we reached Karin's classroom. The way the two of them were discussing my situation made me feel like a specimen in biology lab.

"Never mind," I said, waving good-bye to Nancy and Karin. "It doesn't matter anyway."

"Sure it does," Nancy insisted. "The more you know about what's going on, the better you can deal with it."

"Not this time," I said. "So let's just drop it, okay?"

"Drop what?" Nancy asked. I laughed, wishing I could forget the subject as easily as she had pretended to. But whether Jeff was avoiding me or not, I was determined to talk to him.

Since Karin and I had finally made up, I had done some serious thinking. Jeff hadn't been very understanding about my feelings. On the other hand, he'd been as straight with me as he could be, and all I'd done in return was mistrust him. But even though we didn't see eye-to-eye on everything, I still liked him for the same qualities that had attracted me to him in the first place.

That meant we at least had to talk. It wasn't as though we didn't have enough IQ points between us to figure out a solution to our problems. If we really cared for each other, we could work things out. If we couldn't find some solution, that would prove we really weren't meant for each other, anyway.

At least that's what I was telling myself. Deep down, I knew I still cared strongly for Jeff.

All afternoon I kept watching for him between classes. When Karin and I walked out of history, I still hadn't seen him. "I give up," I said, not even bothering to conceal my frustration. "I guess I could phone him tonight, but he'd probably refuse to take my call."

"I think you are mistaking how he feels toward you," Karin said. "If he avoids you, it is not because he dislikes you. He only wishes to avoid more trouble for you and him both."

I groaned out loud. It would be nice to think that Jeff was not trying to upset me, but he couldn't have picked a worse way. "So, what am I supposed to do?" I asked. "Go to his house and camp on his doorstep?"

"That is possible," Karin said, looking sympathetic and amused at the same time. "But if I were you, I would camp first outside the boys' gym. Jeff always has basketball practice on Mondays now." A smile spread slowly across her face, and she reached out to squeeze my hand. "I think he would not miss the practice for anything—even to avoid this nuisance of a girl Vicki."

"You're wonderful!" I said. "Why didn't I think of that myself?" I wanted to throw my arms around Karin and hug her, but she was already hustling me down the hall. "Hurry up," she said, "or you will be waiting for him until practice is over."

"Thanks," I said as we stepped outside. "I don't know what I'd do without you."

"Without me, I think you would not be in such a mess to start with," Karin shot back. We both laughed, and then I dashed off toward the gym.

After I'd waited outside the main door for ten minutes, I began to wonder if Jeff was already inside. Then I saw him walking toward me, his letter sweater draped casually over one shoulder.

"Hi," I said as soon as he was near enough to hear me.

He stopped and eyed me suspiciously. "Hi. Looking for someone?"

"Yeah, you. I came to apologize. Can we talk for a minute?"

For a moment, I thought Jeff was going to

say no, but finally he smiled and shrugged. We walked over to a wooden bench a few yards from the main door, but neither of us sat down.

"So," I said, "now that we're here, I don't know where to start."

"Neither do I," Jeff said. "I've been thinking about you, Vicki. But I'm not sure if there's any point in talking. I've always been totally straight with you, but you never believe anything I say. I'm not used to being called a liar, you know."

From the way he said it, I could tell he was really offended. I'd been so caught up in my own feelings that it hadn't occurred to me that Jeff was hurt, too. In fact, I'd assumed that he and Karin were both happy—until I talked to her yesterday and saw what a jerk I had been.

"I didn't mean to call you a liar," I said. "And I'm really sorry my words came across that way. Karin and I talked about what happened Saturday night, and I know I wasn't being fair. I'm not used to being jealous, and I'm not exactly proud of the way I've been acting. But you didn't do a lot to help matters, either."

"Oh?" Jeff said, narrowing his eyes. "Other than spending my whole life swearing that I wasn't in love with Karin, just what was I supposed to do?"

I glared at him, feeling the now-familiar angry flush rising in my cheeks. "You could have been a little more understanding," I said, struggling to keep my voice calm. "A lot of girls probably would have felt jealous in my situation. I mean, I was really looking forward to spending Halloween with you at Newport. Being sick was disappointing enough, without having to think of you and Karin having fun without me."

"I know that," Jeff said. "And, believe it or not, I was as disappointed as you were. I've already told you that Karin and I weren't exactly 'having fun without you.' I hardly saw her the whole weekend. That's why I don't understand what got you so upset. You seemed to feel that if you couldn't go, nobody should. I'm sorry, but that strikes me as pretty selfish."

"Oh, sure," I retorted. "Naturally that's what *you'd* think. But some people might think *you* were the selfish one. I suppose it never occurred to you or Karin to stay home and keep me company."

A peculiar glint came into Jeff's brown eyes, and he glanced away in confusion. "No, that didn't occur to me. For one thing, Halloween at Newport is a family tradition. For another, you started coming across like you thought you had a right to choose my friends and run my life." Jeff shrugged helplessly. "Listen, Vicki, I like you a lot, and as I said, we've had some good times together. But when someone starts telling me whom to see and where to go, I start feeling suffocated. Whatever happens between you and me, I'm just not willing to give up having girls as friends."

"I never expected you to stop being friends with girls," I replied instantly. "But I don't want to be part of a three-headed monster, either, whether the third head belongs to Karin or someone else. If we're going to go out together, I need to feel special instead of being treated like one of the crowd all the time."

Jeff's expression suddenly softened. "I never saw it that way. I just like having a lot of friends, and I always feel pressed to include everybody. But you are special to me, Vicki. I guess I haven't been very good at showing it."

When I heard him say that I was still special to him, I felt such a rush of happiness that my knees went weak. But we had liked each other all along, I reminded myself, and that hadn't been enough to solve our problems.

"You can say that again," I said ruefully. "And in a way, I guess, you could say I've been too good at letting you know how special you are to me. What I want to know is, what can we do about it? I mean, you've always told me to say what I really think. But when I do, you tell me I'm a jerk for thinking it."

Jeff stared at me as my message sank in. After a moment, he grinned and threw up his hands in surrender. "I guess I'm not as open-minded as I'd like to think," he said sheepishly. "But it would be a good trick if you could get away with it, huh?"

"Yeah," I replied, trying not to smile. "*If* you can get away with it! So what's going to happen the next time I get jealous and want to spend time alone with you?"

"Well," Jeff said, "first I'll probably say that you're being selfish and unreasonable. Then you'll say the same thing about me. Then we'll put on the gloves and go a few rounds to decide who's right."

"That's not good enough," I said. "I mean it, Jeff. I'm not willing to always be one of the crowd to you. That means somebody will have to get left out sometimes. I don't see why that should be such a big deal, anyway. Even Karin needs some time alone now and then."

"Yeah," Jeff said seriously. "But she needs a friend, too."

I nodded vehemently. "She has at least two of them. You and me. But not necessarily us together. Not all the time, anyway."

At that, Jeff gave me a long look. "Okay," he agreed after a minute. "Hey, you do know that I've missed you, don't you? I heard you were dating Don Bradley."

Inside, I was glowing with happiness, but I just shrugged casually. "Don and I are pals," I said teasingly. "Don't tell me you're planning to start choosing my friends for me."

Suddenly Jeff laughed and pulled me into his arms. "You are definitely the most challenging girl I've ever met," he murmured.

"The feeling is mutual," I whispered back. I locked my hands behind his neck, feeling the warmth of his breath next to my ear and the fluttering of his eyelashes against my forehead. From the day we'd met at the car wash, I'd been enchanted by his expressive brown eyes, mischievous smile, and playful sense of humor. Now when I gazed up at Jeff's face, the same enchantment came over me again. He moved closer, and then his lips pressed against me in a familiar soft kiss. I closed my eyes, melting into his arms and giving myself over to the feeling. The world disappeared as I forgot everything but the strong circle of Jeff's arms and the warmth of his lips.

Suddenly the sound of loud cheers and whistling burst over us like a thunderclap. I jerked away from Jeff and spun around to find the entire basketball team and half the football squad standing near the gym door. My cheeks turned beet-red, and I raised my hands to cover them. Then I saw Don Bradley standing near the front of the crowd, waving his fists in his victory sign. My embarrassment vanished, and I waved to Don.

"See what I mean," I said, turning to Jeff with a grin. "I can never get you alone for a second."

Jeff laughed and bent to kiss the tip of my nose. Then his smile faded and he looked deeply into my eyes. "Seriously," he said, "one of the things I've always liked most about you is that you have a mind of your own. In a way, maybe that's what caused most of the trouble with us. You never seemed to *need* as much attention as Karin did."

"My being independent doesn't mean that I don't need to feel special," I said.

"Well," Jeff said, "I just happen to know about this new pizza place on the other side of town. Why don't you go home and get ready, and I'll pick you up in two hours."

"Great," I said, grinning mischievously. "Karin will love it."

"Nope," Jeff said, shaking his head. "Not a chance, because she's not going to find out about it. There are times to share, but I have a feeling this isn't going to be one of them."

He looked down at me tenderly, his eyes glowing with a soft light. The air around us was eerily quiet. I looked quickly toward the gym and saw that everyone was now gone. Jeff and I were truly alone. I snuggled deeper into his arms, pressing my lips against the curve of his jaw. He turned to capture my mouth in a long kiss, then stood holding me silently.

Then he said, "If you care for me half as much as I care for you, neither one of us should ever have anything to be jealous about again. But whatever happens," he added, tugging my hair playfully, "we'll find some way to work it out."

Yes, I thought, pressing back into his arms, I knew that no matter what happened between us now, we would trust each other and work things out. All our struggles were over.

SWEET DREAMS are fresh, fun and exciting—alive with the flavor of the contemporary teen scene—the joy and doubt of *first love*. If you've missed any SWEET DREAMS titles, then you're missing out on *your* kind of stories, written about people like *you!*

☐ 26293	HEART TO HEART #118 Stefanie Curtis		$2.50
☐ 26339	STAR-CROSSED LOVE #119 Sharon Cadwallader		$2.50
☐ 26340	MR. WONDERFUL #120 Fran Michaels		$2.50
☐ 26418	ONLY MAKE-BELIEVE #121 Julia Winfield		$2.50
☐ 26419	STARS IN HER EYES #122 Dee Daley		$2.50
☐ 26481	LOVE IN THE WINGS #123 Virginia Smiley		$2.50
☐ 26482	MORE THAN FRIENDS #124 Janice Boies		$2.50
☐ 26528	PARADE OF HEARTS #125 Cloverdale Press		$2.50
☐ 26566	HERE'S MY HEART #126 Stefanie Curtis		$2.50
☐ 26567	MY BEST ENEMY #127 Janet Quin-Harkin		$2.50
☐ 26671	ONE BOY AT A TIME #128 Diana Gregory		$2.50
☐ 26672	A VOTE FOR LOVE #129 Terri Fields		$2.50
☐ 26701	DANCE WITH ME #130 Jahnna Beecham		$2.50
☐ 26865	HAND-ME-DOWN HEART #131 Mary Schultz		$2.50
☐ 26790	WINNER TAKES ALL #132 Laurie Lykken		$2.50
☐ 26864	PLAYING THE FIELD #133 Eileen Hehl		$2.50
☐ 26789	PAST PERFECT #134 Fran Michaels		$2.50
☐ 26902	GEARED FOR ROMANCE #135 Shan Finney		$2.50
☐ 26903	STAND BY FOR LOVE #136	Carol MacBain	$2.50
☐ 26948	ROCKY ROMANCE #137 Sharon Dennis Wyeth		$2.50
☐ 26949	HEART & SOUL #138	Janice Boies	$2.50
☐ 27005	THE RIGHT COMBINATION #139 Jahnna Beecham		$2.50
☐ 27061	LOVE DETOUR #140	Stefanie Curtis	$2.50
☐ 27062	WINTER DREAMS #141	Barbara Conklin	$2.50

Prices and availability subject to change without notice.

Bantam Books, Dept. SD, 414 East Golf Road, Des Plaines, IL 60016

Please send me the books I have checked above. I am enclosing $_____
(please add $2.00 to cover postage and handling). Send check or money order
—no cash or C.O.D.s please.

Mr/Ms _____

Address_____

City/State _____ Zip _____

SD—5/88

Please allow four to six weeks for delivery. This offer expires 11/88.